SPELL SLINGERS

STEFON MEARS

Thousand
Faces
Publishing

Also by Stefon Mears

Cavan Oltblood Series
Half a Wizard
The Ice Dagger
Spells of Undeath

Spells for Hire
Devil's Shoestring
Zombie Powder
Spirit Trap
Dragon's Blood

The Rise of Magic
Magician's Choice
Sleight of Mind
Lunar Alchemy
Three Fae Monte
The Sphinx Principle
Double Backed Magic

The Telepath Trilogy
Surviving Telepathy
Immoral Telepathy
Targeting Telepathy

Edge of Humanity
Caught Between Monsters
Hunting Monsters

Power City Tales
Not Quite Bulletproof
No Money in Heroism

Twisted Timelines
Sects and the City
Prince of a Thousand Worlds
Longhairs and Short Tales: A Collection of Cat Stories
Devil's Night
Portal-Land, Oregon
Stealing from Pirates
Fade to Gold
With a Broken Sword
Twice Against the Dragon
The House on Cedar Street
Sudden Death
On the Edge of Faerie
Confronting Legends (Spells & Swords Vol. 1)
Uncle Stone Teeth and Other Macabre Poems
The Patreon Collection, Vol. 1-7 (Vol. 8, coming soon)
The 30-Day Novel and Beyond!

Published by Thousand Faces Publishing, Portland, Oregon

http://1kfaces.com

ISBN: 978-1-948490-36-8

SPELL SLINGERS

CONTENTS

INTRODUCTION

I was a small child when my mother first read *The Hobbit* to me. Her own beloved copy. The way I remember it, she did her best to get me to identify with Bilbo. The little guy, struggling through events that were too big for him and so on.

Maybe it worked. I've always loved that book, and Bilbo is a favorite character for me. But he's not *the* favorite character from that book. Not for me. No. That was Gandalf.

Gandalf knew everything. He wandered far and wide, using his knowledge and wisdom to help others - even if the others didn't always see it that way. And, of course, he had magic.

I wanted to grow up to be a wizard. Just like Gandalf. And I devoured more fantasy tales and more wizards over the years that followed.

From the classics like Merlin to the angst-ridden like Elric to the comedic like Aahz and Skeeve, I read about wizards everywhere I could find them.

From Earthsea to D'Hara to Yurt to Lankhmar to Dying Earth to Discworld and beyond. I didn't care where the wizards came from. I wanted to read about them.

Naturally, I had to write about them too. And you'll find all kinds of wizards in the pages of this collection. Some humorous, some frightening. Some mysterious, some very, very direct. But all of them adventurous, and all of them working wonders that stir the imagination.

Happy reading.

WHEN FLOATING CASTLES DON'T

THEY NEVER LET JAMON GREENSKY ENTER THROUGH THE FRONT DOORS, and don't think he didn't notice.

Apparently the floating castles were too beautiful and impressive to let someone so...

Well, when Jamon was feeling kindly disposed toward himself, he considered his appearance plain and unimpressive. When his mood was darker, he freely admitted that *squat* was the word that best suited him. Gave a sense not only of his height, but covered his overall stature, his limbs, his feet, his hands, his ears, all the way down to the stubby tips of his fingers.

Hell, even Jamon's black hair had a squatness to it. And he knew it.

Add to all that the many scars lingering from his military days and his habit of dressing not in a wizard's robes but in a common tradesman's rough tunic and breeches, and Jamon didn't present the kind of appearance that anyone who could afford a floating castle wanted to let in through the front door.

But they all sent for Jamon, sooner or later.

Someone had to keep those floating castles afloat. And Jamon Greensky was the best at it.

Truth was, he could have afforded fine, dyed silks, an airboat of his own, hells, even a floating castle of his own, if he'd wanted. But he never saw the point in extravagance, and the last thing he'd want to do was become the kind of person who treated people they way the rich treated him.

Right now, for example, they ferried him up to the rear of the castle in a simple wooden airboat – pine wood, with enough space in the flat part for about a dozen barrels – as though he were nothing more than a shipment of wine for the cellars.

And this castle looked as though it probably did have cellars. The wizards who'd first levitated this polished, white stone castle had brought up an entire hillside to support it. So it likely had cellars, and maybe even a dungeon tucked away somewhere beneath its great hall.

But then, this was a grand castle. Often the floaters were small, box keeps with perhaps a tower or two. Something that wouldn't push the spells involved too hard. But this one, this was a *monstrosity*.

Not only was the main bulk of this castle larger than any two reasonably sized keeps combined, this beasty looked to have at least a dozen towers. Plus inner *and* outer walls, which meant courtyards large enough for a tourney while still leaving room for barracks, tradesmen – a veritable village of support for the lord or lady or whatever title this lofty prick held.

And yet, despite the castle's size – and the slight wobble he'd noticed while riding up to the transfer point on his dappled gelding – Jamon could see how every handspan of it, including even the outer walls, seemed to shine in the morning sunlight.

That meant that some poor slobs had to go out there and *wash* those things day after day after day.

Yeah, it was a job. So some family probably got to eat every night because every day daddy or mommy or both went out and risked death to scrub while dangling over a drop of at least a *league*.

Honestly, Jamon would probably just let every one of those stupid bloody floating castles and their arrogant owners come crashing down out of the sky, if it weren't for all the innocent people who'd get hurt in the process.

So Jamon tried to calm himself by focusing on the cool breeze of the ride, the fresh smell of spring on the air, and the view of the farms and villages in the surrounding environs as he rode up in that airboat.

Wouldn't do to start snapping at people as soon as he set down. Whoever met him at the boat, they'd likely just be a poor schlub doing a job. Just like him.

The boat set down on a little wooden dock, built off the back end of the hill, just where the grass stopped growing. The wood was white oak, and stripped and varnished to match the walls. Three other airboats, including one large enough to ferry a team of horses, were already moored to the dock.

Standing stiff as a statue and obviously waiting for Jamon had to be the oldest page Jamon had ever seen. Most often, from what he could tell, page duty was done by the children of nobles, or at least families with money. The kind of job that was part of "fostering," which seemed to be the way the nobles and the wealthy indoctrinated their young with the "way things should be."

Apparently, this one must never have learned the lesson.

Jamon had seen more than two score summers himself, and this guy, he had to have seen at least a dozen more. Had more gray in his hair than black, and more wrinkles on his face than a bedsheet in a cheap inn.

Plus, he was tanned. Nobles tended to look down on that.

Still, the guy was dressed in the livery that said he worked for ... whoever owned this ridiculous excuse for a castle. (Jamon could get the name and title from the formal request for services, but why bother?) White tunic so bright it practically vanished beside the polished stones of the castle wall. Gold trim for the tunic, and for the device that Jamon didn't waste time on.

Red leggings, though, and sleeves, to match the cap on his head. Instead of study work boots like Jamon wore, this page had on short, soft shoes with folded-down collars and likely soles that could get pierced by a moderately sharp rock.

The page didn't look impatient. If anything, the man looked nervous as the tied the airboat to the dock. That was a refreshing change for Jamon as he hefted his pack and scrabbled onto the planks of oak.

Then the wobble came, and the page had trouble keeping his feet. Wasn't much more than a tremor – nothing Jamon would have rated as high as a four on his personal ten-point scale – but it was a sure sign that the spells keeping this castle in the sky were weakening.

"Don't worry," Jamon said, giving the man a smile to try to offset the effect of his voice. Jamon had taken an arrow to the throat back in the wars. Normally, he enjoyed the effect of his rough, grinding voice on the people who both hired and looked down on him. This page, though, he wasn't likely in a position to look down on anybody.

"I've been doing this a long time," Jamon continued, "and the wobble isn't too bad yet. Should be plenty of time for me to right things."

The page cleared his throat. A bad sign.

"Maintenance Wizard Jamon Greensky," he said, in tones as formal as any herald, "I am Albrecht, fourth assistant to the seneschal of High Lord Gerron Brandwraith."

Albrecht paused there, as though just the high lord's name was supposed to make Jamon titter or bow or some other damned thing. But Jamon was too busy realizing that this situation was worse than he thought.

He'd been expected a page to take him to the seneschal or major-domo or whatever. Instead he'd been fobbed off on the seneschal's *fourth* assistant. As though Jamon were no more than a merchant delivering the regular monthly wheat.

Irritation rankled through Jamon's system and made him snort out a breath like an angry horse.

Albrecht continued anyway.

"I am to be your liaison in this matter. I shall—"

"Yeah, yeah. You'll get me to the right place, answer my questions and see to my payment, right? All while making sure that nobody *important* even gets a chance to notice me?"

"Well," Albrecht said with a disapproving frown, "when your work is complete I'll be conducting you to the seneschal's second assistant, Rosalind, at the high lord's treasury, for payment. But other-wise, I believe you have hit upon the essentials."

Albrecht looked Jamon up and down with a clear air of disapproval.

"And, of course, your discretion is appreciated."

Jamon sighed. This was going to be one of *those* jobs.

He almost turned around. Almost got back into the airboat and headed back down for the dock below and his gelding. He didn't need the money enough to put up with this kind of treatment. Espe-cially not from some "high lord" so fancy his seneschal needed at least four formal assistants.

But just before Jamon could turn away, he saw a series of ropes go out over the walls. Coming down those ropes, along with buckets and brushes, were youths, to do the day's scrubbing.

Youths. A dozen of them. Suspended over a league-long drop on nothing more than a length of wound hemp.

Jamon couldn't let this castle fall. Too many innocent lives depended on him keeping it afloat.

Damn it.

———

ALBRECHT MIGHT HAVE BEEN ONLY THE FOURTH ASSISTANT TO THE seneschal, but at least he seemed to know what he was about. Once Jamon was off the docks, Albrecht led him inside the castle through a sally port, and down a concealed flight of stairs to a warren of passages that networked all about the first level down.

No white stone down here, and it hadn't been *swept* recently, let alone polished. Cold, gray stone and the smell of must, rats, and ... was that old sweat?

Well, there was also the smell of pitch, but that was inevitable down here. No spells were wasted on lighting these narrow passages. Instead, torches burned every hundred paces or so. Far enough apart to let the shadows play between them, and leave most of Jamon's hike in an uncomfortable semi-twilight.

Jamon's stubby legs had to work double-time to keep up with Albrecht's strides, but Jamon had been dealing with that particular hardship most of his life. He had more than enough breath to ask, "So, Albrecht, is this high lord of yours at least good to his people?"

Albrecht stopped walking so abruptly that Jamon barreled the poor guy down before he could stop himself.

"I beg your pardon?" Albrecht said, his voice so snooty he might have been looking down from atop some fancy destrier instead of looking up from a bed of dirty gray stones and clutching his fallen hat.

"Well, I—"

"First of all, Gerron Brandwraith is not *my* high lord, he's *every-*

one's high lord, yourself included. Second," – and here he refused Jamon's hand and started making his own way back to his feet – "I'll have you know that life under High Lord Brandwraith has never been better for anyone. Yourself included."

Jamon frowned, and shook his head, but he didn't say anything as Albrecht started up his quick pace again.

Before long, he'd led Jamon to the western cornerstone, where Jamon could finally get to work.

The cornerstone was a crystal of onyx even taller than Albrecht and even wider than Jamon. It tapered toward the top, and had jade-set runes carved into all four sides.

This Gerron Brandwraith may have been Albrecht's favorite high lord, but this castle had clearly been afloat for at least a century. Its spells were designed according to the old style – four corner anchors and a keystone in the center. Not nearly as efficient as the more recent spellwoven-net approach, but generally easier to maintain.

At least, for easier someone like Jamon, who had a knack for the older styles of magic.

The onyx crystal was still spinning sunwise, which was good. It was spinning slowly though, and the glow of the runes was weakening. The jade runes should have shone a bright orange counterpoint to the green of the jade, but they'd faded to more of a dull, red-orange.

Straightening out the glow and the spin rate, those would be simple enough for Jamon to fix. The question was *why* these problems had crept in. The magic of the four cornerstones might not have been efficient in most regards, but once those spells were in place, the cornerstones worked off a kind of feedback loop, each reinforcing and strengthening the others.

This sort of decay was the symptom of a deeper problem.

"Albrecht?"

"Yes, Maintenance Wizard Greensky?" Albrecht still sounded wounded by implied offence given his beloved high lord.

"Call me Jamon. And does y... I mean does High Lord Brandwraith employ a court wizard?"

"High Lord Brandwraith is pleased to retain the services of no less a wizard than Kiramund herself."

Kiramund... Kiramund...

Oh, yes. Jamon remembered. Kiramund was a big deal a few years back because she'd discovered a way to conceal the presence of an entire battalion of troops by magic alone, or something like that.

Honestly, Jamon didn't care much for the kinds of magic he didn't do well.

Still...

"Kiramund dabbling in summoning these days?"

"Certainly not."

Or not that anyone would tell the seneschal's fourth assistant, at least.

"She have any apprentices?"

"Two, Sir—"

"Don't need the names," Jamon said, waving a hand to try to stop Albrecht's certain recitation of names and titles or whatever. "Two. All right. Does the high lord employ or allow any other wizards within the keep?"

"Only yourself," Albrecht said, one eyebrow high, as though the answer should have been obvious.

"Look, Albie," Jamon said, and Albrecht paled at the nickname, "something weird is going on with your levitation spells. I'm just trying to figure out—"

"My name is *Albrecht*, and are you saying the problem is beyond your skill?"

"One," Jamon said, holding up fingers to count each point he made, "no, I'm not. Two, you better hope I can fix this, because there isn't anyone better at what I do. Three, I'm trying to keep it from happening again, so if you could please extract the damned halberd that *someone* must have shoved up inside you and talk to me like a human being and not a nuisance, *maybe I'll be able to keep all your people from dying.*"

Albrecht started to say something about three times, and each time he stopped himself. Finally, he nodded once, and said, "The high lord has banned the practice of summoning. Only Kiramund and her apprentices practice any magic within the castle on any regular basis. Do you think a visitor could have done something?"

"Doubt it," Jamon said, studying the spin of the crystal. "The sort of problem I'm looking at requires time to bring about." He frowned and turned to Albrecht. "Unless you've had a wizard visiting for, say, at least a season within the past half-year?"

Albrecht shook his head. "We have had no such visitor. Could it be one of the high lord's enemies?"

"Not likely, but not impossible. It would mean they'd have had to sneak in a wizard who lived here in disguise and worked magic without the court wizard knowing."

Albrecht shook his head again. "One of Kiramund's regular duties is monitoring for the unexpected practice of magic."

Jamon almost – *almost* – asked a number of follow-up questions there about privacy and techniques and a number of other things that didn't really matter to what he needed to do.

"I want to get this one straightened out before I look at the others. Should make the rest of what I have to do easier. While I'm working would you double-check with Kiramund for me? Just to make sure?"

Albrecht bit his lip as if to hold in an objection, but nodded and turned on his heel to go at once.

And Jamon got started on his repair work.

The worst part about repairing this sort of decay was that it couldn't be resolved with anything quick and simple. It required a three-incense blend, powdered chimera heart, and use of the wand Jamon had forged from the thighbone of a takatiel, a breed of small dragon whose entire life is spent airborne.

Most of all, it required time and patience. Building up the spells just right to contain the power that was already present, and then begin channeling back in that would slowly re-fire the glow of the runes, then gently rebuild the spin rate of the onyx crystal.

Too fast would risk the harmony of the cornerstones. Too slow, and he would waste precious effort when he still needed to check three other cornerstones, plus the keystone.

But Jamon's understanding of timing and pacing were as thorough as his command of the ancient chants, which rolled off his tongue as though he'd been born speaking the tongue of old Rendalla.

As a final step, Jamon added his own discovery – a flourish that would act as a shield, preserving this cornerstone from decay.

The flourish would only last until sundown, but that *should* be just enough time to repair the rest of the spells.

When he finished, Jamon mopped his brow and turned to Albrecht, who regarded him with the patience of the long-suffering.

"Kiramund has confirmed that only herself and her apprentices have worked any magic in the past two seasons. Excepting, of course, the work you do today."

Of course the answer couldn't be that easy.

***

THE SAPPHIRE SERVING AS NORTH CORNERSTONE WAS IN A SIMILAR state. It's widdershins spin rate had slowed, and its jade runes had dulled their glow to orange-red as well. The same could be said for the widdershins-spinning quartz crystal in the east, and the sunwise-spinning ruby in the south.

Whatever had brought about the decay in the levitation magics, it had hit all four cornerstones equally.

That was equal parts good and bad. It was good, in that – because this castle floated through the old system and not the newer mesh approaches – the more or less equal distribution of the drain worked *with* the reinforcing feedback loop instead of against it.

It was bad in that the whole system was much worse off than the wobble indicated. Jamon knew that, even as he finished casting his preservation flourish on the ruby of the final, southern cornerstone. If all four of the cornerstones were being drained equally, then the drain had to be coming from the keystone.

And nothing should have been able to interfere with the magic of the keystone.

Jamon was mopping his brow and gnawing on a piece of jerked beef during a vital moment of rest after finishing with the last of the cornerstones.

This part of the undercastle wasn't quite so bad. It must have been closer to the storerooms, because the smells of must and rats were noticeably less present. Instead, the air smelled drier, but cleaner.

The passages here were lit by oil lamps, instead of torches, and Jamon could tell that someone had even swept recently.

Jamon was just trying to decide if that meant visitors actually came down here sometimes, or if it meant that the area he'd started in had been closer to the dungeons, when something happened that shouldn't have been possible.

The great ruby cornerstone's spin slowed.

Just a hair. So little that Albrecht must not have noticed. Because when Jamon's jaw dropped – along with the rest of that strip of beef – and he stepped right up to the spinning ruby, Albrecht asked, "Whatever is the matter?"

"The keystone," Jamon said, snatching up his pack and forgetting all about his snack. "Get me to the keystone. *Now*."

For once, Albrecht didn't question him. Just took down one of the oil lamps before turning and leading Jamon through a concealed door and into a passage so tight that Jamon's shoulders continually bumped the gray stone walls.

Albrecht set an even harder pace now, but Jamon only pressed him harder, trotting on the taller man's heels to get him moving.

The passage sloped ahead of them, and Albrecht took a series of turns through side passages at intervals that looked random to Jamon. But the seneschal's fourth assistant must've known what he was doing, because he finally stopped in the middle of a T-intersection.

Instead of turning left or right, Albrecht pressed a series of stones until one clicked. A section of wall slid away to the left, revealing a sharp slope down into a rough, chasm at what had to have been the lowest point in the hillside attached to the floating castle.

The chasm spread out like the bottom of a bowl. Here the dirt had been fused by fire magics into a clay as hard as good stone. And floating in the air above the base of that bowl, the keystone.

The keystone was the petrified heart of a dragon. Large as an ox, it was, and golden in hue. Traced all about its length and breadth were runes, not engraved, but impressed using rarest heart-of-jade.

No torches or lamps down here, save the one that Albrecht carried. But none were needed. The keystone itself provided the light.

Light that should have shone out bright as noonday sun, but right now only glowed with ghostly witchlight. The sort more likely to float in a swamp and lure travelers to their death than to light up any sky.

And the keystone – which should have been immobile – rocked back and forth in the air.

The problem was worse than Jamon thought.

"How long have you known about the problem?" Jamon asked.

"Well," Albrecht hedged, but blanched when Jamon turned a fierce look on him. Abashed, Albrecht continued, "the first signs were three weeks ago. We sent for—"

"Don't care who," Jamon said, waving away what would no doubt be a list of more presentable but less able maintenance wizards who considered themselves Jamon's rivals. "Did they do any good? Or did they make things worse?"

"Well, I hardly think—"

"No politics," Jamon said. "Just give me facts so I can figure out how bad this is. Please."

Must've been the please. Albrecht swallowed, and spoke much more candidly.

"Truthfully, they took their money, but I'm not sure they accomplished anything. They promised that results would—"

Jamon waved off that answer.

"So, no, they didn't make anything better. But did they make things worse?"

"I ... don't think so."

"All right," Jamon said, thinking as fast as he could. "What prompted contacting me?"

"The high lord was awakened by a tremor on the eve of important negotiations involving..." Albrecht cleared his throat. "The high lord was roused from sleep."

"So that was the strongest shake?"

"Yes."

"That would be ... three days ago?" When Albrecht nodded, Jamon continued, "And how often have the tremors come since then. A few hours apart?"

"After the high lord's awakening, they came perhaps a quarter day apart. But their frequency has increased to about what you say."

"Wait," Jamon said suddenly. "What was this you said about important negotiations?"

"Well," Albrecht said, getting formal again, "I hardly think that—"

"I don't need details, but I need to know this. Was the court wizard involved?"

"Certainly not."

Jamon frowned. Something or someone had been draining the keystone for power. Not easy, in and of itself, but far from impossible. Still, why would...

"The other party involved in the negotiations. It wasn't Kiramund's homeland, was it?"

"No."

"What about her apprentices?"

Albrecht paused. "I ... don't know."

"Bring me Kiramund. Not for aid, but for answers. If anyone questions, tell them it's a matter of keeping this castle floating or letting it crash, and I'm not kidding."

Albrecht turned at once and started running.

Jamon drew a deep breath, and regarded the keystone.

"All right, baby," he said as though speaking to a wounded animal, "show me where it hurts."

Repairing the magics of the keystone started like a normal repair job. Jamon used the right incenses, the combination of the takatiel wand with a second wand he'd made by weaving and petrifying strands of hair from the tails of four unicorns.

He'd even done the chants in the older style, with the two-tone throat voice he tried to avoid around witnesses. It had sounded scary enough *before* he'd taken that arrow to the throat. These days, he sounded downright demonic when he did that voice.

But the usual steps were not enough.

Oh, the runes had restored to their proper glow, and the heart itself shone out now like ... at least late-morning sun, if not proper noonday.

But the keystone should have floated with the stillness of a mountain's core. Yet Jamon's clever eyes could detect the faintest tremors that would grow all too soon into a real problem.

He paused to look around for Albrecht and Kiramund, but they had not arrived yet. Irritating, especially since Jamon had been working here for ... at least a couple of hours. Dusk would fall all too soon, and the preservation spells he'd cast on the cornerstones would fall with it.

If he didn't resolve this soon, the cycle of decay would start all over again.

All right. What did he know? He knew that something was draining the keystone, and through it the cornerstones. He knew this was not normal decay, because he'd resolved all normal decay issues, and done the right spells to restore full functionality to the levitations of this floating castle.

So another spell had to be tapping into it. And Jamon would have to find that tap and break it.

This was *not* magic he was good at. This was modern, intrusive magic, and most of the concepts behind it tended to confuse Jamon.

So he had to think about it differently.

Suppose this castle had added something. Perhaps an external floating bunker. And they attempted to add...

No. The details of the analogy didn't matter. And what the

intruder was doing with the stolen power didn't matter. What mattered was how the intrusion interacted with the system.

That, Jamon could figure out.

There was a spell tapping into the keystone, as though it were ... as though it were a *fifth* cornerstone. Only it wasn't properly established in the network, so it didn't work with the feedback loop, and neither gained nor provided reinforcement.

It was a pure drain.

But if it were to function, even theoretically, as a fifth cornerstone, it would have to be...

...straight above.

Jamon snatched up his pack, stuffing things in as quickly as he could while he hustled out the door and made his way back through the passages under the castle.

He kept the darkness at bay with the faint glow that came from his unicorn-tail-hair wand, which shed a silvery light when all around was black.

Fortunately, Jamon didn't have to worry about which side passages to care about. He just needed to keep going up the slope at every turn, and before long he was back by the southern cornerstone, where the ruby was already spinning a little slower than it should have.

But Jamon understood why, now. His preservation spells would aid against the normal cycle of decay, but couldn't help against a drain that came from within the system.

No time for that now. He was in a cleaner portion of the passages, which meant there had to be stairs up somewhere around here.

And people...

Jamon hustled back and forth, looking for doors and shouting for people. Before long, a young serving girl in a short, gray frock turned the corner in front of him, going from irritated to aghast the moment she saw him.

"Stairs," he said. "I need to go up."

"This way," she said, recovering herself better than most, and not even averting her eyes from Jamon's admittedly disturbing appearance. She led him through a few more turns, and then pointed him to stairs.

"Do you know where the throne room is?" Jamon said, gambling that the makers of any castle this extravagant would put the throne in the literal center of all things.

"Of course," she said, "but—"

"No time for objections," Jamon said, waving away her words. "I need to get to the throne room now, or this whole castle may fall before dawn."

Alas, Jamon could only *wish* he were exaggerating. Whatever drain was taking power from the keystone, it would be getting an influx from Jamon's work. And that could result in the drain reaching for yet more power, in a far more dangerous kind of feedback loop.

To the serving girl's credit, she nodded and turned to lead him quickly up the stairs.

The main floor of the castle was the same white stone as the exterior, and just as clean. No rushes for this place. Oh, no. Clean floors and large sections of red carpeting. Ornate tapestries for the walls, and lamps that glowed with the light of sunspells, not flame.

Guards in chainmail and carrying spears looked puzzled at Jamon as he passed, but the presence of a known serving girl must've been enough to set them at ease, because they didn't challenge him. Not until he reached the throne room itself.

The serving girl vanished with the skill of all lower workers once she'd gotten Jamon to the throne room, so when the two men standing guard moved their spears to bar Jamon's path to the large, closed double-doors, no one stood by to help him.

"I need to go in there."

"No, you don't," one of the guards said. This one stood a little taller, and had a slightly longer beard, so Jamon figured he had to be the senior guard.

Plus, he was the one who'd spoken.

"Do you have family here?"

"You threatening me, scarface?"

"Not even a little," Jamon said. "But if I don't get in there, you'll die, along with your family, your high lord, and probably everyone not just in the castle, but within the nearest dozen farms and villages. I mean, have you ever seen on of these floating castles fall? It's not pretty."

"What are you talking about?"

But the guard next to him raised his spear and shoved the other guard's aside.

"Gina's pregnant," he said to the first guard, who frowned at the news.

"We can't just let him—"

"You telling the truth?" the second guard asked. The one with the shorter beard.

"I'm Jamon Greensky, and there's no one who knows more about keeping castles floating than I do. And I'm telling you that this castle will fall if I don't get in there."

"Good enough for me," the second guard said, and opened the door.

For such a massive hall, it was remarkably empty. There were rows and rows of seats along both long sides, but no one sat in them. The floor in here was laid with pale blue marble, interspersed with white, as though to replicate a sky with scant clouds. The ceiling above had been done the same way, and behind those rows of seats, high windows angled to show the sky above the walls, as well as letting in bright sunlight.

Someone who must've been High Lord Brandwraith sat on his throne. The high lord was younger than Jamon would have guessed. No more than a score of summers had passed since his birth. But he certainly dressed the part of a high lord, with his colorful silks, and the gem-encrusted circlet of gold adorned the soft brown hair on his head.

Standing beside the high lord was Kiramund. Tall and regal Kiramund in a simple robe of rich blue silks. She might have been older than Jamon by perhaps two-score of summers, but she carried her years better than he did, with her straight back and her lustrous white hair.

Standing before the high lord, on the second step of the four that led up to the high lord's dais, was ... some emissary or other. He had the bulk of a man who knew where his next meal was coming from, but his clothes were finer than most merchants bothered with. And from his posture, Jamon thought this emissary objected to having to stand in an empty great hall, when whatever business they conducted could have been handled in a smaller, more comfortable room.

Off to one side, frustrated, stood Albrecht, who turned an apologetic expression on Jamon the moment he saw him.

The high lord and his guest did not look up from their hushed conversation, but Kiramund raised her eyebrows at Jamon.

Jamon started forward, noticing that a gentle, flowery smell grew stronger, the farther he got into the room, from faint and barely noticeable to ... likely strong enough to protect the high lord from the odors of his court.

Typical.

Jamon was about fifteen steps from the dais when the high lord looked up.

"I don't recall sending for a..." Brandwraith frowned. "What exactly are you?"

"This is Maintenance Wizard Jamon Greensky, excellency," Kiramund said, turning her eyes on Jamon as she continued, "though what he could be doing in *here* I couldn't begin to guess."

"Really!" the emissary said. "This is the final straw. Send for me when you are ready to take this matter *seriously*."

The big man left in a huff.

High Lord Brandwraith raised an imperious eyebrow at Jamon.

"I trust you have a good reason for setting back important negotiations?" he said, in tones that implied a visit to the dungeons if he didn't like Jamon's answer.

"Believe me, High Lord Brandwraith," Jamon said, "the last thing I wanted to do was come in here. But I sent for your court wizard and she never came."

Of course, Jamon might've needed to come here anyway, since he couldn't count on Kiramund having the answers he needed, but he was still irritated that she hadn't come.

"It is not your place to send for me," Kiramund said. And she might have said more, but the high lord waved her to silence.

"Why, then, are you here?"

"Someone has managed to tap into the levitation magics that keep this castle afloat."

"And you suspect me?" Kiramund asked, her voice dripping with challenge.

"No," Jamon said, shaking his head. "You'd know better than to mess with the older style levitation magics. But *someone* tried to fake a fifth cornerstone in the system, to drain its power for other purposes. And I've traced it here."

"Why here?" the high lord asked.

"Straight line to the keystone?" Kiramund asked.

Jamon nodded. "Which means..." He stopped and looked at the high lord. "With your permission, of course."

The high lord nodded, and Jamon knelt under the throne.

Took him only a moment to find it, affixed to the bottom of the high lord's seat. A piece of gold jewelry, encrusted with onyx, quartz, ruby and sapphire, with jade runes. Just touching it, Jamon could feel how it tied into the keystone, and from there the cornerstones.

"That looks like Ronnel's work," Kiramund said, studying the spells woven into the jewelry.

"One of your apprentices?" Jamon asked.

"Of course."

"Is he from ... whatever place you had some kind of important negotiations w—"

"Ronnel's from Valsta?" High Lord Brandwraith said.

"He is," Kiramund said with a sigh, "but I hadn't realized he still had divided loyalties." She bowed low. "Please accept my humblest apologies, your excellency."

High Lord Brandwraith nodded. "You will deal with it then?"

"I will." She turned to Jamon and extended a hand.

"Sorry," he said. "You can have this in a moment, but I need to cut it free from the system first, then verify that there are no aftereffects."

Kiramund looked as though she wanted to object, but the high lord said, "Of course," in a firm voice.

Jamon then dug into his toolkit for something he rarely needed – a dagger with a ebonwood handle and a copper blade edged in dragonscale and tempered in the misty blood of three ghosts.

With his right hand he pulled the blade from its hard leather sheath, and immediately the air buzzed with its power and gained the faint odor of blood.

He didn't like having to use this particular tool. It was just too dangerous. Even holding it jangled his nerves and sped his heart. But unweaving these spells in a regular way might take time the castle couldn't afford.

"*You* have a ghost blood dagger?" Kiramund asked, managing to sound offended. "*I* don't even have a ghost blood dagger."

"It's not for sale," Jamon said, not sparing enough attention to note her reaction to his taunt. The ghost blood dagger was very tricky to wield.

He held up the enchanted jewelry in his left hand.

He tapped first the gold of the main part of the jewel, using only the tip of the dagger. He listened within the buzz for the slight shift of the contact on deeper levels. When the buzz gained a slight overtone in a higher pitch, Jamon knew the dagger had touched not only the solid gold of the jewel itself, but the deeper layers of spellwork woven into it.

He then repeated the touch to the jewels corresponding to the cornerstones, in the reverse order he'd repaired them earlier. Each time, he waited for the telltale shift in the overtones of the buzz to indicate contact at the deepest levels.

The ghost dagger could cut through almost anything, but only in the hands of the patient and skilled wizard. If he rushed, if he didn't wait for all the right connections to be made, when he went to cut, the dagger would find first the connections that kept him alive.

With all five contacts made, each on the three deeper levels of enchantment, Jamon slowly pulled the dagger to one side.

High Lord Brandwraith began to say something, but Kiramund, to her credit, shushed him.

With a single, swift movement, Jamon cut the air beneath the jewel with the physical part of the dagger while its magic devoured the spells of the jewel, severing it from those of the keystone and its cornerstones.

The dagger's buzz faded, replaced by a warming hum. The dagger at its most dangerous. Fed once, it would seek more food unless put back to sleep.

Jamon dropped the jewel and picked up his sheath. He spoke soothing words to the ghost blood dagger in the tongue of old Rendalla as he eased it back into its sheath.

"Please tell me you lain the proper spells on that sheath," Kiramund said.

Jamon didn't dignify that question with more than a glare as he wrapped the sheathed dagger in black wool and replaced it in his pack.

Only then did he allow himself a deep, cleansing breath and the chance to mop his forehead and, hopefully, bring his heartrate down to something like normal.

He sat back on his heels, wondering when he'd knelt.

"Is the matter resolved, then?" High Lord Brandwraith asked.

Jamon nodded. "I'll need to double-check the cornerstones and keystone, to be safe, but that should take care of it."

"And you say that this ... this totem" – the high lord pointed at the no-longer-enchanted jewelry – "was the source of the problem?"

"Absolutely," Jamon said, and Kiramund, perhaps not to be outdone, chimed in with, "Unquestionably."

"Then I shall not only forgive your intrusion, but see to it that you are given a bonus of..." The high lord tilted his chin back and forth as he thought. "...twenty percent."

"Your excellency's generosity does him credit," Jamon said, amazed that he didn't choke on the words. Probably because of what he needed to say next. "But there is something I need more than a bonus."

"And that is?"

"Apprentices."

"I see," the high lord said, raising one eyebrow as though deciding on the value of an apprentice.

"I can't keep doing this forever, and I need students who haven't been..." – don't say corrupted – "trained in the modern systems."

"Perhaps Ronnel..." Kiramund started, but Jamon cut her short.

"No. I want youths who have no training in magic, so that I can guide them along the proper lines." He frowned and pointed at the fallen jewel. "Besides, anyone who did this once might try it again. I won't have it."

"I note your use of the plural," High Lord Brandwraith said.

"You seem to have an abundance of youths washing your walls. In place of the bonus your excellency has offered, I'd like to select four of those youths to take on as apprentices."

Of course, that those youths would no longer be engaged in daily, high-risk work was a bonus unto itself.

The high lord favored Jamon with an imperious glare.

"Those who wash my walls and castle are already employed, and being trained to serve in the castle. They are not yours for the asking."

"Never mind then," Jamon said, hefting his pack. "I'll take my payment and leave. However, the next time your castle wobbles, don't bother calling for me. I won't come."

"I beg your pardon?"

"Send for another," Jamon said, knowing full well that no other maintenance wizard could have done what he did today. "And hope they're good enough to keep you in the sky."

"How *dare* you?"

"Look at it this way," Jamon said. "If your castle supplies my apprentices, whose jobs will they give priority to in the future?" Assuming they'd been treated well here, of course. "It's in your best interest."

"Your excellency," Kiramund said softly, "today this man *did* save your life, and the lives of all who live here."

"Oh, very well. Make your selections, take your payment, and begone with you. And, Albrecht!"

Albrecht hurried forward so fast he probably wrenched his neck on the bow.

"See to it this man is conducted everywhere he needs to be *unobserved*. And whether or not he's made his selections, I want him on the ground below by dinnertime."

"Yes, your excellency. Right away, your excellency."

Jamon actually spared the high lord a bow, then let Albrecht lead him to a concealed side door.

After all, he was well used to being shuttled about behind the scenes. Just one of the things he'd have to teach his apprentices to use to their advantage.

NOT A MAGIC THIEF

I don't steal magic, Your Majesty. Well, not often, anyway.

I'm not saying your Royal Wizard is a liar. I'm just saying he's *misinformed*.

All right, look. I got bounced out of my apprenticeship because I couldn't just *accumulate* magical power through meditation or some other crap. Yeah, I can get enough to do the little things all on my own, but I could never gather any real power and hold it inside me.

No, I don't know why. My master didn't know why either, and neither did any of his six – *six* – other apprentices.

Yeah, I don't think any of them tried very hard to help me on this one. Especially my competition. Excuse me, "fellow apprentices." I got caught one time – *one time*, Your Majesty – just borrowing a little power from Urella and that was it. It was just waste from her spell anyway. She was never very efficient, and you'd think I'd get credit for my ingenuity.

But no.

Suddenly two years of study and progress meant nothing. I was out on my ear with only the lime green linens of an apprentice on my back and a sack of food for my walk of shame back home.

So Deveran the blacksmith's son became Deveran the failed wizard instead of Deveran the Mighty, or any of the other sobriquets I'd come up with while practicing spells. But blacksmithing wasn't much an option for a runt like me. I mean, look at me, Your Majesty. Not much taller than a fencepost, and let's be honest. Not much wider either. These supple, slender fingers couldn't straighten a nail to save my life.

That's the crime, if you ask me, Your Majesty. The way I was tossed out by my master. Look at these dark, piercing eyes, my strong jaw, my onyx hair and widow's peak. I was *born* to be a wizard.

Anyway, obviously, I didn't go home. My path led through a forest with a reputation for being haunted, and the next thing I knew I'd found an old log cabin where a witch used to live. And by "used to" I mean I found a dead witch. Gray and wizened, and well, she stank like she'd been dead a while. Stank bad enough that I didn't even consider trying to move in and take over the place.

Shame, too. It would have been a nice home for a little guy like me. Cozy and well-built, with a feather bed (which is where I found the witch), tons of herbs hanging from the ceiling to dry, and a nice cauldron in the center hearth. Even found a little roast boar meat when I gave the place a casual once-over, not that I could have stomached it.

But I did find two useful things in that little cabin. Note the key word there, Your Majesty. "Found," not "stole." The witch was already dead, and it wasn't like there were any relatives beating down the door to claim what she had. So all I did, really, was keep these things from—

Of course, Your Majesty. The point of this is that the old woman had been more than a little sloppy in her spellcasting, and she'd left years of accumulated magic hanging in the air. Enough that if I hadn't done anything about it, the place would have really become haunted. Maybe scared a few woodsmen or innocent girls on their way to their grandmother's house with lunch. Maybe something worse. So really, I was doing everyone a favor. Collecting all that magic.

And stuffing every vim of it into this gold amulet. Didn't see that tucked under my shirt, did you, Your Majesty. Not the kind of thing I like to advertise. Beauty, though, isn't it? Solid gold sun for the pendant, I think, with the three great jewels of magic: snowflake obsidian, garnet, and sapphire. And...

Your Royal Wizard's disbelief aside, Your Majesty, I studied quite hard under my former master, and I do, in fact, have a strong hold on the magic I learned. I just ... had trouble doing anything about it.

At least, until I found this amulet. It stores magic, you see. Which is how I went from Deveran the failed wizard to Deveran the hedge wizard, with a shot at one day becoming Deveran the Mighty after all.

I had a goal now. I had purpose. I needed to go to the old places, the wyrd places, and collect all the magic I could. See, that's what I'm talking about, Your Majesty. I'm more like a ... magic recovery specialist. Not a magic thief.

What I do, it's basically a public service.

And if I hadn't been out recovering magic this fine spring day, I never would have been near that ruin when it all went down.

THE GUARDS WERE TELLING ME – NICE GUYS, THOSE GUARDS, BY THE WAY – that the ruin marks the border between this country and Dainiskan. I didn't know that at the time. All I did know was that back when that ruin was a castle, the great wizard Gord the Maker had made it his home for some three centuries. Sounded like a potential treasure trove of leftover magical energy, just waiting for me to come collect it.

It was even better than I expected.

The leftover magic stretched all the way from the ruin, across the mile or so of rough, blasted rocks and all the way out to the edge of that great pine forest. Whatever brought that old castle down had to have used enough magic to wipe out your castle and probably your capitol city too, and more than a stretch of surrounding countryside.

Oh, no. No, no, no. I'm not saying anything like that, Your Majesty. Don't mean any threat at all. I'm just trying to give you a sense of scope about what must have happened, way back when. Whatever took that castle down, that was bigger than anything even my former master could do.

No, I wouldn't presume to speculate about what your Royal Wizard could do.

Now, out at the edge of the forest there wasn't a lot of loose magic, but I had nothing *but* time. The sky was clear, the bluebirds were singing, and I had a belly full of roast rabbit and more waiting in my sack for dinner.

So I started just after dawn, and slowly worked my way in, just gathering up the loose magic, likely the remains of that old attack, and stuffing it into my amulet.

Probably around noon when I got to the ruin itself. That castle must have been something, back in its day. Looked as though it was shaped out of reddish granite, and probably glinted in the sunlight.

But all the tall towers were fallen. And the parapets, the two outlying walls, the great castle itself. All of it, just smashed like so much rotted fruit. The ground was dry and rocky around the ruin, but the debris was so thick within the ruin itself, that I never did see the ground.

Stone dust dappled the air, and tasted so dry I must have gone through three water skins between noon and dusk, picking my way through the remains and gathering spare magic.

Eerie kind of quiet there. Only saw a pair of crows all afternoon, and they didn't alight nearby, or even caw. Just flew past overhead, like even they didn't want to hang around this old place.

Nearly lost my way twice, because even smashed as the castle was, large, scattered chunks of reddish granite still stood about twice my height.

I had to clamber over some of them to get deeper in. You see, Your Majesty, the closer I could get to Gord's old tower...

Of course, Your Majesty.

I spent the whole day gathering power there, and by the time dusk was approaching I still hadn't found Gord's tower. I could feel it nearby, but I couldn't get close enough to begin to tap into it.

So I planned on staying the night, and continuing the next day.

I was too tired to realize what it meant when I found the clearing. It was just a big slab of reddish granite without any cracks or uneven spots, broad enough that I could have built two or three of that witch's cabin on that slab and still had room to walk between them.

I was too tired to think about the fact that someone had to have cleared this area. To realize what the lack of dust meant. Or maybe it was just that I figured I was the only person anywhere near the ruin.

Didn't need a fire. My food was already cooked, and I had plenty of light from the waxing moon and stars above. And between the three of us, a fire would have cast shadows that might have gotten spooky. I'd been a little worried that Gord the Maker had left enough loose magic when he died that, after all these centuries, it might have formed a haunting, so I didn't want any dancing shadows when I lay my head down to sleep.

Dancing shadows were what I saw when I woke up though.

The moon was high in the sky when I realized my eyes were open. My head was a bit fuzzy, but living on my own and largely outside for a few months had bred some caution into me. Before I could make sense of what I saw and heard, I'd rolled over to the nearest up-jutting chunk of debris and tucked myself into it.

Voices. I could hear voices. Couldn't make out their words yet. Too many echoes. And I could see flickers of yellowish light, smell the burning pitch of torches.

I'm not sure what I was dreaming about before I woke up, but I remember staring at the flickering light and shadows along other up-juts of rock and thinking that there *was* a haunting and it was coming for me.

So I tucked in a little farther. Not that I expected it to help.

But then I found out it wasn't a haunting.

It was men entering the cleared area. Armed men. From two directions.

Now, remember, Your Majesty. It was dark, and these torches were spoiling the adjustments my eyes had made to the moonlight. So I couldn't see sigils or standards.

What I could see was that there were two groups of five, and they all looked like men to me. But some of them were in armor, so I can't be sure of that.

In fact, both groups broke down the same way, as though the groupings had been arranged in advance. Three in armor, chain and boiled leather, sheathed swords, and loaded crossbows in their hands. One man holding a torch. One wizard.

Yes, I'm sure about that part, Your Majesty. You see, any wizard can always spot another wizard by the echo of power around them, and—

Yes, Your Majesty. What matters here is that I'm sure each group had a wizard. They were young, though. Barely any beards, and I think they were still in the blue robes of journeymen. Again, to remind Your Majesty, hard to be sure in that light.

Nobody pointed a crossbow right off. The folks in armor kept their weapons pointed high. The wizards faced off as though each were waiting for the other to make a move.

That's what I'm talking about, Your Majesty. That is what passes for a wizard these days, your Royal Wizard excepted, of course. In their boots, I could have—

Yes, Your Majesty. I'm sorry, Your Majesty.

Where was I? Right. The torchbearers turned out to be the two most important people there. One was a big man. Not fat, but solid, like he was born with a lance in his hand and had been fighting ever since. Short hair, combed back, and it looked grayish in the torchlight, which made sense with the lines in his face. Had a big cloak on, too, with the hood down.

The other wasn't much bigger than I am. Taller, maybe, but just as thin. Long, long beard though, and it looked black as night in the torchlight. Had a long, crooked nose too. I remember staring at it for a moment. No cloak for him, but his garb looked fancy, like it was made from cloths I couldn't afford.

Are you all right, Your Majesty? Should I call for ... oh. You know who those men are. Don't you? No, you're right not to tell me, Your Majesty. Better I don't know.

Anyway, I had to crouch back farther into the shadows because the crossbowmen started looking around for potential targets, and I sure didn't want to be one. So I couldn't quite hear what the torchbearers were saying. They kept their tones hushed anyway, and deep as the big man's voice was, every word he was saying got swallowed up by the granite.

Every word until one: Treason.

He bellowed that word, so sudden and sharp that one of the crossbowmen loosed. Nearly took my head off.

Then they were all shooting each other, crossbowmen screaming and falling left and right. The one who'd loosed drew his sword, which was good for Crooked Nose, because the big man drew a sword of his own and then the night was ringing with steel.

But my focus was on the wizards. They were pulling together enough raw power to obliterate every living thing within an arrow's flight, including me.

So, I made an exception to what is usually my hard-and-fast rule.

I reached out and stole the power from both of them before either could cast and I shoved it into my amulet along with the power I'd been accumulating all day.

Great move for my immediate survival. Bad move for surviving the next several minutes.

You see, Your Majesty, I didn't have time to be subtle, like I'd been as an apprentice, nipping little dribbles of magic from people like Urella. I had to reach out and pluck it before they finished casting.

So they felt it go. And they could feel right where it went.

And while the swords were clanging and someone was yelling, two journeymen wizards turned and gave me looks as though they intended to show me just what I'd failed to learn when I got bounced out of apprenticeship.

Well, I didn't have a lot of time to think. I had to act and I had to do it fast. And maybe this sounds strange to you, Your Majesty, but I was thinking about you too. I mean, the big guy had yelled "treason," and that sounded like something you needed to know about.

So I took every vim of power I'd accumulated all day and shunted it into the only spell I could think of. A traveling spell, intended to convey me smoothly and gently from my little hidey-hole and straight to your royal castle, where I could present myself and tell you my tale.

Your Royal Wizard is right to scoff, Your Majesty. It was too much spell for me, but I had accumulated so much power I could try it anyway.

And as you saw, it didn't quite work right.

Anyway, Your Majesty, this is how I came to be standing at the foot of your royal bed this fine night, and please let me apologize once more for interrupting you and your royal consort.

He's quite lovely, if you don't mind my saying, and he's quite gentle-hearted as well. Please convey to him my thanks for talking you into hearing me out here in what I hope is a tiny audience chamber and not my future cell. And if I may say, your ermine robe is quite becoming.

Anyway, that's all there is to my story. And every word of it is true, even if your Royal Wizard – who looks smashing in his fine red robe, which quite complements his excellent silver beard – wishes to paint me as a magic thief.

Which I am not.

That's all there is to my story, and you obviously recognize the players involved, so I'm sure you and your Royal Wizard have a great deal to do. A great deal that doesn't involve me, so I'll just let myself out, shall I?

AND TERROR GAVE HIM WINGS

Even the rushing waters of the river seemed to call Garran a failure.

The gentle blue stream he'd followed from the tower first widened angrily as it approached the canyon. Now here at the canyon's edge, it bent hard over rocks, frothed white, and mocked him with its deep hiss as it plunged down the grays and browns of the cliffside. Foam spat at him, chilling him even more than the last breath of winter had done all morning.

Garran had left the tower shortly after dawn. Now the sun now rode high in the bright blue sky. Garran's undyed roughspun shirt and pants were already half-wet with sweat from the long hike to get here, and the leather bag slung over his shoulder was sealed with a spell. The spray from the river made him no more wet as it mocked.

Garran knew no spells to quiet the river. He knew one to call water *from* the river, but from the look of this place that would be the last thing he'd want to do here.

Ahead of him, the trail down was more rock than dirt, and those rocks were wet. The way steep. Not sheer, but steep enough.

Still, "canyon" seemed too grand a word for this gash in the green, hilly countryside. True, Garran had never seen much of canyons, but from the maps he had read he had imagined grand, sweeping places filled with yellows and reds as much as browns. Rough stones pocked with holes that could be ground away with the hilt of a dagger to mark his passing.

Instead, what Garran saw looked no more than twice the width of the river, and the river was yet narrow enough to ford with a single good elm. The canyon floor looked as muddy as rocky, and the shrubs that grew from the cliff walls and canyon floor looked stunted and sparse.

Yes, it extended a good few leagues. Still, it seemed that this was as much as canyon as Garran was a wizard. Perhaps it was a mere apprentice as well, with aspirations that may never be fulfilled.

Perhaps, then, the canyon would have mercy on Garran when he made his descent. See in him a kindred spirit.

He had no noble's solid boots, but Garran's shoes were leather, with good soles. His master, the great wizard Darreon, always made sure his apprentices were well-shod. But even good soles could slip on wet rocks. Garran was slender and quick, but he lacked the sure feet of Darreon's youngest apprentice, Simi, who seemed at times to be half mountain goat.

And those rocks had edges that looked unforgiving. Pointed in places. Jagged in others.

What an end that would make for Garran. Slain not by some dragon or great foe, but by the sharp edges of rocks on a long, painful fall down a canyon that barely merited the name. Garran, the oldest of Darreon's three apprentices — this year would mark his twentieth summer — and the least tattooed with his deeds.

Today was the third day of spring. Today Darreon heard the song of the year's first swallow north of the Everwhite Mountains.

The day of trials.

Today should have been a day of triumph. And it would be. But not for Garran.

Today Darreon would test two of this three apprentices: Tahaz and Simi. Those two were ready. Their scalps already tonsured clean, while Garran was allowed no more than to cut his black curls short and shave away his whiskers.

When they passed their trials, Tahaz and Simi would gain the final tattoos of the apprentice and the first of the wizard. Already the ochre swirls and dips of their accomplishments spread up their arms to their shoulders. When they donned the vest of a wizard, their readiness would be plain to all with eyes to see. For no artist could fake the tattoos of a wizard. They spread only through the magic of his achievements.

Garran's yellow silk vest sat waiting in his trunk, along with the matching silk pants and simple leather sandals he would wear the day he was anointed a wizard. But they would wait for some time yet. Garran's tattoos barely extended halfway from his wrists to his elbows.

Which was why Garran was ordered to spend the day of trials gathering reagents. Scouring an apprentice canyon for stillwheat, a rare herb which grew only from the roots of shrubs that burst out through cracks and fissures in rocks. It was hard to spot, because it grew to match the color of the bark nearest it, but its texture was stiff and sharpish, like wheat. Stillwheat anchored and preserved its host shrubs during the cold winters and died out through the spring to disappear entirely by summer.

He would be fortunate to fill his pouch by sunset. Garran might well have to seek shelter for the night and return to his master's tower in the morning.

Garran considered that for a moment as he gazed down the cliff-side at the flatter, muddy gray and brown stones that formed the bottom. Perhaps Tahaz and Simi would be gone by the morrow. Off chasing tasks they set themselves now, rather than those set by their old master. If Garran did not return before tomorrow, he might not have to witness their glory, listen to their triumph.

Garran sat right where he stood on the wet stone. He opened his leather bag, pulled out a dull red apple and a chunk of sharp cheese sweetened with almond oil. He held up the apple, mouth open wide to take the first bite, then grimaced.

Darreon could have sent Garran out for the stillwheat yesterday, or the day before. The first day of spring might have been the best day to gather it, in terms of available quantities. But Darreon had sent Garran out today.

This was a test. A test of his mettle. Did Garran have the dedication to gather and return today, knowing he would suffer facing the triumphant elevation of two younger apprentices? Or would he take the easy path and return on the morrow to spare himself the humiliation?

Garran sighed and stuffed his lunch back into the bag, sealing it with an aspirated word of power.

Perhaps Garran had spared himself too many times.

He stood and started down the rocky incline.

The easiest descent Garran could see did weave back and forth down the sharp slope, but tightly, as though for the ease of goats, not proper pack animals. And if it had ever been a true path then no one had maintained it since the days when elves still walked this land. The rock sizes were irregular, and their colors varied from reddish through deep brown to gray, and all of them darkened by spray from the falling river.

The smaller rocks shook under Garran's weight. The larger stones, though, were too slick. Some kind of slime grew, fed by the river's spray.

By the time Garran had descended ten feet, he'd slipped twice.

At the second turn, he fell.

This turn was closest to the river, spray thick enough here to sop his hair to his brow and stick his roughspun to his chest. He had his feet apart for balance, inching across a wide gray stone covered in a slick white fuzz, trying to aim his weight at a thick red rock that could prove to be his salvation. This rock looked almost dry, positioned somehow that half of it avoided the river spray. And at the edge of the rock jutted a sickly brown limb of a shrub with maybe a dozen tiny, furled green leaves.

Just the sort of shrub where stillwheat grew.

And Garran had his mind on the stillwheat, not his footing. And when the cliff suddenly shook, Garran couldn't hope to brace in time.

His left foot slid first, but his right was quick to follow. He slammed down on his side. His air *woofed* out of him. A miracle he'd tucked his head, or that might have been all for Garran.

Instead his body slid fast across the slick fuzz, aiming for a quick, painful trip down to the canyon floor. Not at the red rock with the shrub but at a jagged outcropping, wet and gray and evil-looking.

Garran's lungs froze from the blow. His belly quivered, trying to breathe but nothing would come. And without breath, no spells could save him.

The edge came at him fast.

Garran yanked the pouch from around his shoulder. Flung the strap at the shrub and prayed to any god who might be listening that this shrub was locked in place by stillwheat.

The strap hooked over the shrub.

Garran slipped over the side of a nasty rock. Its jagged edge ripped his roughspun and tore open his side.

But the shrub held.

Garran hung there against a slippery gray stone, trying to get air back into his lungs. He clutched his pouch for dear life, and hoped that the shrub and the strap would buy him time to think of something.

———

WHEN HIS LUNGS FINALLY REMEMBERED HOW TO BREATHE, GARRAN first smelled something foul. Rancid. Like an animal left to die some-place warm and wet. The smell gagged him, almost to the point of retching, but just that much shaking of his body flared out pain from the gouge along his back, between his right shoulder and hip.

Garran shook, shivering in the cold spray from the river falling beside him. He kept gagging from the odor, grateful that he didn't have his apple and cheese to vomit up. Small consolation for a man clinging to a leather bag to avoid sliding to a painful death.

He heard a sound. Deep and grinding, like two boulders twisting together.

But the sound wasn't coming from the cliff. It was coming from the air behind him.

Garran risked a glance, and immediately wished he hadn't.

For what he saw was a giant.

The giant stood at least eight times the height of a man. Its skin was pale and chalky, but its wooly hair and beard black as night and wild around its head, which was close enough to reach out and bite Garran. The giant's jaw was heavy, and jutted out past its nose, which looked to have been smashed flat more than once and finally crum-pled into place. More black hair matted the giant's chest and, thank-fully, its loins.

It stood, one huge, horny foot on each of two separate boulders perhaps half the way up the canyon. One hand leaned against a large reddish rock, and the other held a gray stone club that was at least as long as Garran's whole body.

But the giant himself looked skinny. The giants Garran had read about — and the one his master Darreon had told of — were massive, nearly as broad as a tower turret. But this giant was barely broader than two horses side by side.

Whatever Garran was thinking, it was washed away by the foul odor of another rancid giant breath.

Another rumbling sound, but this time Garran was ready for it. He had little more than a smattering of the speech of giants, but their language was hardly the most complex tongue to be found across the face of the land.

Garran should probably have been terrified. Certainly, if anyone had told him this morning that sometime close to mid-day he would be wounded and hanging from a cliff when he met a giant, he would have stayed in bed and suffered the consequences of disobedience.

But Garran discovered that his fear had a limit, and past that limit appeared to be a sense of calm. He could only hope this wasn't the peace of death settling in. Not yet.

"That twig," said the giant. "Too weak to hold you."

But calm or not, speaking past this much pain was not easy.

"There's ... a secret ... great one."

"Ho!" laughed the giant, pointing at Garran's arms with his club. "Ho, ho! Tattoos. Wizard."

"Yes ... I—"

"Wizard. Taste like lizard. Good eating."

The giant reached for Garran, but no spells that Garran knew could piece that thick hide.

But maybe he didn't have to.

"*Wait!*" he yelled.

The giant grabbed Garran by the shoulder and hefted him. It was the left shoulder at least, and Garran felt a moment of relief when the muscles of his right side stopped straining to hold him in place. He managed to hold onto his bag, which came free from the shrub as the giant lifted him.

The giant lifted his club to deal a finishing blow.

"*Wait!*" Garran yelled again.

"Why?" said the giant, brow furrowed as though the interruption was taxing its mind. "High sun. Best time to roast wizard."

"Why eat one human when you can eat a dozen?"

The giant's eyes narrowed in suspicion. Its massive head turned this way and that.

"Where? Where more manfolk?"

"Up there." Garran pointed with his left hand. His side was throbbing and he worried how much blood he was losing.

"Ho! Ho, ho! Little liar." The giant shook its head. "No way up, little liar. Steep. Slippy."

"But there *is*." Garran pointed to the shrub. "Wizards know the shrub's secret."

The giant's jaw worked. More grinding noises.

"I can make your feet sticky like the shrub," said Garran. "You can walk up the slippery rocks. Walk to the world above and eat all the manfolk you like."

"Little liar," said the giant, shaking its head. "No way up."

"I can prove it."

That made the giant look at him.

"I can do the same to my shoes. I'll walk up and you can follow. I'm small. I could never outrun you once we reach the top."

The giant's nose flared, and Garran knew it could smell his blood.

"Yes, I'm hurt too. I'll be an easy meal and you'll be out of the canyon. And I'll get to live at least a little longer."

The giant licked its lips with a cracked tongue.

"All right, little wizard. Make your magic."

"There's something I need to make it work..."

THE GIANT HAD A DEN UNDER A JUT OF GRAY SHALE. THE DEN SMELLED even worse than the giant's breath, if such a thing were possible. It smelled of more raw meat, but there was a groove in the rock where the giant relieved itself, and the pungent stench of that clung to Garran's mouth.

The giant had lined the edges of its sleeping area with the bones of its kills: goats, mostly, but more humans than Garran liked to think about.

The giant's bedding was a pile of rank goat hides, but too thick to be goat hides alone. Garran guessed that within the pile were the skins of humans as well.

No fire anywhere that Garran could see. He wondered for a moment how the giant planned to roast him. Then decided he didn't want to know.

And he had higher priorities.

First, he dug a salve out of his pouch and did his best to smear it over the rent in his flesh made by the jagged rock. With each touch of the salve, cool relief began to spread. Purely a temporary measure, alas. The salve would cleanse the area, stay the bleeding, and help the flesh begin to knit. But the damage was done, and the muscles and skin would remain hurt until Garran healed.

Days, thanks to the salve, instead of weeks, but days he didn't have.

The giant's belly rumbled like distant thunder, low and constant. Garran's own empty stomach couldn't bear the thought of food. Not with the riotous odors assaulting his nose.

Just as well. The giant was impatient.

As soon as Garran explained what he needed, the giant began ripping up every tiny shrub and hint of bush it could find. And the giant could cover a lot of ground. It brought back handfuls of shrubs as fast as Garran could find and clear the stillwheat from the last batch.

And with each batch, Garran shook his head. "Not enough," he said each time. "Not enough."

And with each batch he stuffed more of the stillwheat into his bag, until he had all his master had asked for, and maybe a handful more.

But the giant's eagerness for an endless meal of manfolk wore quickly through the impatience of its rumbling belly.

"How much more?" it demanded, when the pile of shrubs beside Garran was tall enough that he no longer wondered where the giant would get its firewood.

"We have enough," he declared, clapping his hands together.

Garran was glad he'd had a chance to salve his back, because as hard as his heart was pounding, he might have bled out without it. If he failed one way, he died. If he failed the other, he died, and caused the death of countless others of his own people before the giant was stopped. Sweat stung his eyes now, but at least he'd grown used to having his roughspun sticking to him everywhere it touched.

The giant picked up its club and loomed Garran into shadow

Garran separated the brownish-graying stillwheat into two piles, a roughly eight-to-one ratio based on the amount he expected to need for his own shoes. He gathered up his own pile, half in each hand, and sat cross-legged on the stone floor of the giant's den.

Garran whispered the right words across the stillwheat, his own breath carrying the magic into them until they glowed a soft yellow.

The giant made a deep, appreciative sound that might have been satisfying to Garran, under other circumstances.

Garran held the stillwheat to his shoes and it clung.

"There," he said, standing. "Mine are done. Now lie down with your feet facing me."

"You sat."

"I am small. The magic is brave with me. But you are mighty, great one. Spells fear to touch you. You must lie on your belly to show the magic you mean no harm. Then it will feel safe to enchant you."

The giant narrowed its eyes, but lay on its belly, great stone club in hand. The giant watched Garran over its shoulder.

"No tricks. Smashed wizard tastes good too."

"No tricks," said Garran. *Not about this part anyway.*

Garran gathered up the remaining stillwheat, separating it into two piles and hefting one in each hand. It seemed like enough for a dozen mounted knights. It might be enough for a giant. And it had to be. In his current state, Garran could never outrun that club.

Once more he breathed magic onto the plants as he said the right words to enact the essence of the stillwheat into the steadfast-footing spell. The piles glowed yellow, bright enough that Garran had to look away.

He cringed from the rough texture of the giant's foul feet, but at least his nose seemed to have no room for more horrid odors. Either that, or the giant's feet were the best-smelling part of it.

But Garran smeared almost all of the remaining enchanted stillwheat into place on the giant's feet.

"The spell is done, great one. Come, follow me up the canyon wall."

And without giving the giant time to stand, Garran turned and ran.

The wet rocks did not slip under his shoes now. Even the slime seemed to almost grip his soles as Garran ran as fast as he could manage.

Behind him the giant roared and rumbled to its feet. Dozens of steps behind Garran now, though. Scores, perhaps.

Garran was quick. Normally. But today he was tired from the long hike to get here, and wounded from the gash on his side. His body needed rest and food, neither of which he had time to give it.

But Garran did have terror. Plenty of that. And terror gave him wings.

But the giant's strides were worth at least a dozen of Garran's. As the two of them raced up the side of the canyon wall the giant gained.

And gained.

The river spray all but blinded Garran, but he kept his feet pounding. Behind him he could hear the giant's thunderous footsteps, shaking loose stones. Off to Garran's left, a small avalanche began.

But not where Garran needed it. Not between him and the giant.

The top was coming up fast. Garran's heart raced faster than his feet. He panted for breath. Exhaustion burned through him. His wound began screaming. Must have opened again.

The giant's club *whooshed* past Garran's head.

Garran screamed and leapt for the top ledge.

His hands gripped the ledge. The last of the enchanted stillwheat stuck his hands to the top of the rock. The grip helped him sling himself over to land hard on the stone.

The giant's arms came over the ledge.

Garran whistled the words to release the spell.

The giant's feet slipped free. But its hands gripped the stone.

The wet stone.

The giant's hands started to slip. It howled. Let go of its club and Garran watched the giant's fingers begin to dig right into the stone itself. Any moment it would find a grip. Any moment it would pull itself over the ledge. Any moment Garran would be dead.

Garran threw his hands at the river and sucked air through pursed lips, inhaling with all the force his exhausted lungs could muster while his tongue worked the shape of the spell he needed.

A jet of water gushed from the river and into the face of the giant.

In shock and surprise, the giant let go. It tumbled down the rough and jagged rocks toward the canyon floor below.

Boom.

The ground shook with the impact.

Garran crawled to the edge of the canyon and looked down. The giant sprawled on the rocks below, still moving. As Garran watched, the giant shook its fist at him. It tried to roar, but the sound was weak.

Garran hoped the giant had broken bones, at least.

He rolled onto his back again, enjoying the warmth of the afternoon sun, and the fact that he may yet live to see tomorrow.

Garran pulled off his roughspun shirt and applied more salve to his back. He was right. The wound had re-opened. But he could rest a while now, and eat, before he returned to his master's tower.

Garran was re-donning his shirt when he saw his arms. The tattoos on his arms stretched to the elbows now. Was it the spells? The quick-thinking? The duress? Garran wasn't sure.

One thing he did know. When he saw Tahaz and Simi tonight, he would congratulate them.

And after he did, Garran would have a story of his own to share.

BIND BY THE RIVER

THE EXHAUSTED RIDER SLOWED HIS HORSE TO A WALK AS DUSK BEGAN TO gather about him. The forest and safety tormented him with their distance, within sight now but hours ahead. He knew they would fade as the horizon shrank with the setting sun. He stumbled from his saddle, lay in the road where he fell while his chestnut brown gelding moved off to munch wild grass.

Terlik envied the horse. He had no food for himself, nor focus enough to trap some with magic after the long day's hurried ride. With all speed he had to carry his message to the Forest People. They would shelter him, feed him. They would even take him in and continue his training while Terlik's master, Gord the Maker, dueled his rival. They would take over and complete his training, Gord had assured Terlik, should his master lose.

But just then their ancient spells hid in that fading forest, along with food, and safety. Terlik had none of those things, for the kings of Yastil had long ago decreed such restrictions on all messengers. Officially their lack of weapons and provisions proved that they were not spies. Unofficially it was said that Naaron the Third of Velstadt first proposed the idea to ensure that messengers did not tarry in their duties.

Whatever the reason, for Terlik it meant that the Forest People would question the veracity of his master's message if Terlik arrived armed or well fed. The use of small spells to skirt this restriction was overlooked for wizards – even apprentices – but Terlik had spent more time with books than on horseback, and he felt that lying on the rutted, broken dirt of the road matched the level of exertion he could still attain. The red clay would not stand out against his hair when he met the Forest People, and perhaps not even against his dusky skin, if he had but time to brush himself down before delivering his master's words.

Terlik considered simply sleeping where he lay. Surely he could expect no riders by night, not when he had passed an inn only two hours past. His stomach grumbled at the thought of that inn: rich, thick stew with tiny globules of fat shimmering on the surface, rye bread so thick it must be dunked before chewed, the tang of the local salt beer....

Where did his horse wander off to?

Terlik sat up, groaning at the sad state of his abused muscles, but he could not see his horse. Had it gone north toward the foothills or south toward the ... what lay south? Oh, yes, more foothills. Eagle's Rest Forest grew out of the place where the Giant's Teeth met the Dragon's Spine.

No wonder few seek the Forest People, thought Terlik. *If giants and dragons once dwelt in the great mountains near here, who would wager that they will not return?* His body complained but rose at his urging to a standing position, nearly two yards tall and thin as a twig. Terlik's master even referred to him as Terlik the Twig on occasion, and Terlik devoutly hoped that did not become his sobriquet when he someday earned his staff.

Terlik looked south, then north, but saw no sign of his horse. Perhaps, wiser, the horse had wandered back east toward the inn. "Merlach," he called, then clicked his tongue in what he hoped was the right manner. Whether it was or not, Merlach the horse ignored him, if it heard. Terlik rubbed his dark eyes, his narrow cheeks and high forehead, but could not wipe away his enervation. He was too tired for magic, but he could not risk losing his master's steed. He wished he could rest, just close his eyes for even a little while, but the light had already begun to fade. Terlik needed to find the horse now or not at all.

He stepped off the road and knelt in the Pose of Recompense, decided that he had made the wrong choice and shifted to stand in the Pose of Third Command. But that was wrong too. Terlik hung his head, fatigue wearing at what little focus he had. He ran his fingers over his tight curls, shorn close to his skull. A spell of finding was beyond him. He had to accept this. In the morning, perhaps, he could manage it, if the gelding were still in range, if nothing had killed it and no one had claimed it.

Terlik could not risk that. But what more could he do?

Then he had a thought. He had not the strength for a spell, but the horse might. Had Terlik left any binding stones in his saddlebag? Alas, no, they were all in his pouch. Still, Merlach was his master's horse, his master's rightful property. Terlik was his master's apprentice, given the horse in trust on a sworn task. If the horse were Terlik's, the bond of ownership would provide connection enough to tap the horse's strength for a small spell. Perhaps Terlik's connection to his master and his further connection to the horse – at least for this task – might create sufficient bond for an enchantment to take. Terlik rubbed his neck and considered. If the connection proved too tenuous, then given his current state, Terlik could likely look forward to intense pain followed by unconsciousness lasting until at least midday. But what choice did he have?

Terlik scraped a narrow sliver off of his flint with his hunting knife, the closest thing to a weapon any messenger was permitted. In his hand Terlik mixed the sliver with ground leaves from the hallah tree and a pinch of caro root. Over these he said the right words in Chaldish, the tongue of ancient Chalda Before the Fall, though his tongue stumbled as pressure from the spell rose in response to his words, beat through his chest, locked his limbs rigid until only his mouth could move. Even sweat could not drip down Terlik's forehead as he chanted, however much his pores wished to cool his skin, grown fever-hot from his casting.

Were Terlik fresh and relying on his own resources, this simple spell would not have pressed him so, would have been finished and done in a single verse with no noticeable effort. But now the apprentice strained through three necessary repetitions: once for him, once for Merlach, and once for the bond. When the final syllable fell past Terlik's numbing lips, the mixture in his hand flared and soared off to the north. Terlik gasped at the release and stumbled forward to his hands and knees, panting. Sweat now drenched him as though the tidal wave had broken the dam.

But he would find Merlach now, even under cover of darkness, for the horse would glow white with witch fire. Terlik could afford to sit for a scant few minutes. Perhaps even rest his head...

Terlik heard a decidedly human yelp come from the north,

possibly the sound of a horse thief shocked at the sudden glow of his quarry. Terlik longed for a brief moment to let the thief have the horse and continue on foot. But Gord would expect Merlach's return, and Terlik would be held accountable.

The apprentice moaned and forced his awkward way to his feet.

§

The horse itself might be easily found – even now Terlik could see the witch fire's glow crest a slope a few hundred paces ahead of him – but the distant light did nothing to ease Terlik's path in the deepening dark. Away from the road the ground grew rough, dried and broken by summer heat, though the rains of fall were only a week away, if Terlik had read the portents correctly. The moon above shed little light to aid him, hidden at this time of month down to a bare suggestion of itself. Every step challenged the weary apprentice and he nearly fell three times, including once that almost brought him down on a snake, which hissed a warning but wanted nothing to do with him. Terlik could not see it clearly, but he would have sworn that the snake's belly swelled in the middle from an early dinner.

Even the snakes have food, he thought with a grimace.

The slope, when Terlik reached it, could not have risen more than twice his own height, but he resorted to scrabbling up on all fours, as though climbing a rock instead of hiking an inconvenience. The slower speed lent him stealth, and as he neared the top Terlik heard two distinct sounds. The soft chuckle of a stream thrilled his parched lips, drier even since his spell. But he forestalled his eager rush forward at the second sound: a soothing voice, as of one calming an animal.

A horse thief? One that would steal even a wizard's horse? No one could mistake the witch fire for anything other than spell work, so this thief had nerve and experience. And probably a weapon. While Terlik had no sword – just as well for he had shown little aptitude for the weapon – only a hunting knife he could do nothing with beyond skin game and prepare tinder. Terlik's minor host of spells lay beyond his current reach. He knew he could not even have managed a second witch fire spell without sleep, to say nothing of any enchantment strong enough to hinder a horse thief.

But the thief did not have to know that...

Terlik took a deep breath, drew himself to his full height with as much dignity as he could manage, fixed his face with what he hoped was furious rage, and strode to the top of the slope, doing his best to ignore the protests his body made at every step.

§

As he reached the top Terlik felt his expression crack. At the foot of the slope, Merlach's reins in hand, crouched a warrior. She looked lean, deadly and half-crazed by the light of the witch fire: eyes narrow and a roguish scar set off against her dark cheek, her long tight curls wild and almost alive as she moved. Curved sword at her side and pliant, strong hide armor to protect her, Terlik knew he would present no more than a momentary distraction if he got in this woman's way. He would have to bluff his way through this. Terlik tried to imitate the tone he had heard his master use to command spirits.

"Step away from my horse, thief, and I might—"

"I'm no thief," she said, never looking away from Merlach. Her gentle tone seemed intended for the horse, but her arched eyebrow lent threat to her words. "And I've almost calmed your horse down after your thoughtless spell, so have a care."

"But—"

"My own horse is hobbled not two hundred paces north of here, where I intended to camp for the night. Make your next words respectful and you may share my fire." She met Terlik's eyes with a dead expression, as though further disrespectful words would prove fatal.

Worse, Terlik felt certain she could see his eyes, though she stood close to witch fire and Terlik dozens of paces away, shrouded by rising night. Terlik slumped, shoulders, knees and neck, too tired to continue his charade. "Thank you for finding Merlach," he said, "and for the invitation to share your fire. I am called Terlik, apprentice to Gord the Maker."

Though he kept his tone as polite as he could, he must have said something wrong, because he noted a tightness around her eyes and lips.

"You named your horse Merlach, after the ancient king?"

"My master named him. He says kings would rule better if others held their reins."

"Very well." She stood and let Merlach's reins fall. "I am Vonetta called The Swift. Once Captain of His Royal Highness Draven the Fifth's personal guard, now disgraced sword for hire. Now, come dine with me and we will discuss the tasks that bring us out into the night."

"I am not to dine well," Terlik said as he made his slow, unsteady way down the slope. "I serve as a messenger."

"A fool's restriction. Well, a half-portion will not break any oaths or royal decrees. Besides, you may wish to eat your fill while you can. For I have been sent to kill Terlik, apprentice to Gord the Maker."

§

Terlik froze, too few steps from the warrior and her no-doubt keen blade. "I ... I'm a wizard," he managed, his words even shakier than his knees and his heartbeat.

"An apprentice," Vonetta said with a sigh, "and right now not even that. Think, boy, you can scarcely walk much less fight. I may be in disgrace, but even I won't slay the helpless. Now come, let us eat and rest by the proper light of a fire." In a quick movement with her sword hand, perhaps to underscore her point, she grabbed Merlach's reins and held them out to Terlik. "Can you manage two hundred more paces, or should I help you onto your gelding?"

"You're not afraid I'll ride off?"

"Half-dead from exhaustion and hunger on a horse that glows brighter than the moon?"

"Fair enough." Terlik took the reins and Vonetta helped him mount by grabbing his collar and heaving him up. He tried not to think of the cleaving power an arm that strong must have.

They walked in silence, Vonetta guiding Merlach by the bit, until they reached her camp. Terlik wracked his fatigued mind to find some way out of his predicament, but nothing came to him, so he turned his attention to the camp, hoping to spy a way out. Before Merlach's glow faded out Terlik saw four fish on a spit above an unlit fire, near a ready bedroll. A hobbled horse nickered a greeting to Merlach, who snorted something back. Nothing here Terlik could use.

As Terlik managed to dismount and rub down his gelding without help – for which he felt a kind of spent pride – Vonetta lit the fire and poured them each a cup of wine. She sat on her bedroll and broke a chunk of heavy-looking yellow cheese into two not-quite-equal halves. She handed the smaller chunk and a cup to Terlik as he sat on the ground just out of arm's reach.

"To Destiny, the fickle bitch," said Vonetta, raising her cup. "May we love her when she treats us well and escape her when she spites us."

Terlik had never heard that toast before, but drained his cup to its spirit. In a better state he might have consumed half a bottle of wine – even a rich red Hrakashan vintage such as this one – before feeling its effects, but that night he felt the kick almost instantly: lightheadedness, with a hint of sleepiness in tow. Still, his stomach gurgled gratitude for anything at all, and Terlik gnawed at the sharp, heavy cheese while Vonetta refilled his cup and turned the fish.

Terlik fought to stay silent while they ate, and his stomach urged him to concentrate on the fine trout and sturdy cheese. But the wine had its way, and by the time Terlik finished his second fish, he almost slurred when he asked, "Why me? Why would anyone wanna kill me? I'm jus' an apprentice."

"And a messenger." Vonetta's words were quiet, but her tone almost intense enough to sober her listener. "You carry words to the Forest People. Evidently someone doesn't want them heard."

"Bah! 's jus' news and a greeting. I'm half the message." Terlik jabbed himself several times in the chest with one finger. "They're suppose' to teach me while my master duels."

"Are you supposed to tell that to any stranger you meet?"

"Who cares?" Terlik waved his arms. "I'm gonna die!"

Vonetta blinked in thought. "Not just a message then..." Her words so soft Terlik had to lean forward to hear them. "An old alliance..." Louder – loud enough that Terlik jerked upright and fell backwards – she said, "Tell me. Who trained your master?"

"Jodiah, the Sky's Vengeance," he replied from his prone position, in the obvious tone of someone answering the color of the sun. Terlik tried to sit back up, wanted to know why that mattered, but it felt like entirely too much effort. Far better to stay lying where he was. Yes, he would just lie here right where he fell. Surely no rider in the night would trample him. Not so close to an inn....

§

Terlik awoke to the smell of roasting duck. A delightful aroma, but as knowledge of his predicament thundered back, the duck combined with his nerves and forced him to roll to one side and empty his stomach of last night's repast.

"Rinse your mouth in the river," said Vonetta in a gentle voice as she passed one more handful of spices over the spitted fowl. "Then sip a few handfuls to settle your stomach. If that's not enough you'll need some camp bread before you can handle the duck."

Terlik mopped his sweaty brow on his sleeve and pushed to his feet, refreshed at least somewhat from his heavy slumber despite his rude awakening. He felt steadier as he knelt by the river and did as Vonetta suggested. He stood and stretched, and saw that Vonetta had a bow strung and a quiver of arrows next to her re-tied bedroll and a bloody arrow near the fire.

Terlik looked at the Eagle's Rest Forest, still a good two hours ride from where he stood. He glanced at Vonetta, involved in preparing the duck. With direct access to the river from its bank, Terlik could call on a host of spells. Perhaps he could escape, explain the loss of Merlach later....

"Do anything that could be mistaken for casting a spell and I'll put an arrow in your throat before you finish."

Terlik considered whether this could have been an exaggeration, but had to admit that she seemed confident. Too confident. He sighed. He marched back and slumped to a seat beside the fire.

"Why feed me if you're just going to kill me?"

"The duck can do without attention for a moment or two. I could kill you now if you aren't hungry."

Terlik's recently emptied stomach gurgled loud enough for an answer. Just as well, because the tension singing through his body had clamped his jaw shut.

"I thought as much." Vonetta gave Terlik an enigmatic smile. "Even King Draven would not deny a doomed messenger a roast duck leg." She chuckled to herself.

Terlik pulled back from his fear through a single deep breath. A second breath and he had enough clarity to consider his options. This woman meant to kill him, and many a wizard had died at the conclusion to an unprepared fight. But Terlik yet lived, which meant he might find his way through this yet.

"I have money." He dug through his pouch, scooping out a handful of bronze coins and a pebble. The pebble he tossed into the fire, but the coins he held up. "Not much, it's true..."

"More than a tanner's apprentice would have, but not enough."

Terlik let the coins fall back into his pouch, plucked out a second pebble, then turned in disgust and threw the pebble into the river. "Information? We hear many things at my master's tower. Perhaps..."

"Do not die begging like some fat merchant. Die a man worthy of respect. You've lived an apprentice, but you can die a wizard." Vonetta sliced a leg off of the duck and held it out to Terlik. "A fed wizard."

The duck leg was stinging hot in Terlik's fingers, but the savory scent made his mouth water. He enjoyed a juicy mouthful before asking, "Why did you want to know who trained my master?"

Vonetta chewed on a chunk of breast meat that she had speared on her knife, and blinked at the question until she swallowed. "Old rumors," she said. "Nothing that need concern you now."

"Do you know what binding stones are?" Terlik took a small nibble while Vonetta shook her head. "I'm not surprised. Most wizards abandon them once they pass apprenticeship. Personally, I think I'll continue to keep a few on me even after I earn my staff. Useful little things." Terlik relished the pitying half-smile Vonetta gave him at his words' implication but focused on the heat of his duck leg to keep his tone steady. "You see, most spells require some sort of connection to their target. Well, *require* is the wrong word..." Terlik chewed as he thought, noticing that Vonetta now had switched her knife to her off hand and allowed her fingers to move near her sword's pommel. He continued, "But it's like the difference between picking up a horse's tail and picking up the horse."

"And that pebble you threw in the fire..."

"Was a binding stone, yes, like the one I threw in the river. The one you mentioned connects me to the fire, which roasted the duck, which is even now in your belly." Terlik stretched his lips in a smile. "See why I think they're useful?"

"You ate the duck too."

"I could explain the mathematics, if you like, but suffice to say my own spells can't hurt me, even ones that kill you."

"You're bluffing."

"Am I?"

"If you're telling the truth then why haven't you killed me?"

"You've been very hospitable for an assassin. Enough to make me think you really were the personal guard captain for King Draven—"

"I'm not the one with a reason to lie."

"—which means that 'old rumor' you heard might be important to my master. What is it?"

"A snippet attributed to the king's soothsayer. 'When the scion of the sky falls, hope shall hide in the forest.' Typical soothsayer garbage." Vonetta rocked on her shins, and Terlik realized she could spring from that position. "Now, about your spell..."

Vonetta threw her duck covered knife and sprang to her feet, her sword seeming to fly into her hand. Terlik rolled backwards as the juicy missile sailed overhead. He spat two words in Aarkadian, waving one hand like fanning a flame. Damp smoke rushed out of the fire pit, filling the camp with choking darkness. The horses panicked, whinnying and stamping, though hobbled and unable to run.

Terlik, staying low, rolled and crawled toward the fire, certain Vonetta would head for the river. He held his silence for a slow twenty count, then called out, "Throw your sword in the river! Or I *will* kill you!"

Terlik pulled his shirt over his mouth to keep his air that much cleaner, but he knew how low the smoke should get and that, in theory, he was safe. He lamented the panic of the horses, but strained to hear any response from Vonetta. He drew breath to yell again, then heard a splash.

"There," came Vonetta's voice. "I've done it."

"Swear it. On ... on the life of your horse."

Vonetta did swear then, but the oath she snapped out was no promise. Terlik heard a second splash, then, "There! I swear on the remains of my honor and on the life of Duwena my horse that I have thrown my sword in the river."

"Stay where you are." Terlik broke the charm and the smoke dispersed, not that the horses took much comfort from the sudden clean air. Terlik could see Vonetta now, ankle-deep in the river and no doubt close to her sword. Terlik stood and said, "You've seen my magic. You saw me touch the river and the fire through my binding stones. You know I can kill you. Do you agree?"

Vonetta gritted her teeth and gave a tight nod, her wild hair shaking with her rage.

"Then this is the price of your life: forsake your assignment. Keep to your camp here until noon, then go your own way. I'm going to take my horse, and your arrows, and ride on."

"Disgraced as a captain, now disgraced as a sell sword. Perhaps you *should* kill me."

"Perhaps," said Terlik as he calmed Merlach, which did not take long because, though spooked, the gelding was not unused to magic. "But if you wish a third chance in life, ride for the tower of my master, Gord the Maker. Tell him who you are and what passed between us, and tell it true. Then tell him the rumor you told me. I'll be shocked if he does not offer you a better alternative than death."

As Terlik rode off, Vonetta had yet to leave the river. At his last sight of her, she looked contemplative. Terlik hoped Vonetta visited his master. Surely Gord the Maker could see the value in that prophecy, if it held any, and the value in Vonetta, who was perhaps not so far fallen as she thought.

Terlik pushed Merlach harder, hoping to spend both his own and his steed's nervousness through exertion, even though his muscles still cried with soreness from yesterday's ride. He wanted to gain as much distance as he could as fast as he could, in case it occurred to Vonetta that a binding stone might be too crude a tool to extend a thaumaturgic link from a fire to a meal cooked over that fire.

Wizards did abandon the use of binding stones for a reason....

DRINKING AND CONJURING DON'T MIX

"HERE, HOLD MY ANCIENT TOME AND WATCH THIS."

I sighed and rubbed the bridge of my nose, but not because Perry was bad at his magic. A certified journeyman, he excelled at mobility and light spells. Easily a quarter of the nobles and wealthier merchants in town rode in carriages propelled by his handiwork, and lit their gardens, salons and galleries with his artfully arranged enchantments.

"The last time you said that to me, you tried to bring that suit of armor to life."

"Oh yeah," he said as he cleared the space at the end of his work-room. "I probably should have considered that something designed for battle might have violent tendencies. I still can't believe you got that magistrate to let us off with a warning." He chuckled. "Some of the town guardsmen still won't talk to me."

He dabbled in conjuration as a hobby. He had no native gift for the work, but tried to make up the difference in enthusiasm. Perry had plenty of that. He studied *Conjurer's Quarterly*, and purchased relevant grimoires whenever and wherever he could find them. Every time we spoke he was tinkering with some new idea or approach.

He even managed a few successes. For example, he had a familiar . . . if you could call it that. I hadn't been present when he bound it, but as nearly as I can guess from the bits and pieces he'll admit to, he summoned a spirit of creativity or inspiration. Of course, being Perry, he didn't have an animal or homunculus prepared to serve as its host, so he had to improvise.

It was the only familiar chalkboard I've ever seen.

The spirit hated its accommodations. It spent the first month swearing at him without stopping, always in obscure tongues. It had calmed down some since then, but it wasn't ready to be helpful yet. On the other hand, it taught me a few words of Aarkadian that I'd never have picked up otherwise. Not that I could use them in a formal presentation.

Anyway, Perry and I had been drinking some Hrakashan skul I'd picked up from a traveling merchant on his way through to Velstadt. It was my turn to buy for our biweekly game of Crossed Purposes and the strong, bitter skul made us both nostalgic. We'd been laughing over near misses and narrow escapes from our days as eager and impulsive apprentices, when Perry announced that he had a demonstration for me.

Thus, I found myself holding said ancient tome while Perry prepared his summoning circle. Most conjurors still use candles out of a sense of tradition, and in some cases for purposes of ritual harmonics, but Perry was too proud of his light magic to settle for actual flame. At his gesture, the candlesticks glowed deep blue and pale yellow, colors sympathetic to his working, while the circle itself grew slowly lambent with the soft green of purity.

Perry gleefully set out his incense and scented oils before donning a medallion inscribed with what I hoped was the correct sigil. I've always been better at conjuration than Perry, but I prefer working with illusions. They don't require as much preparation.

His chant was Thelmastii, full of sibilance and harsh consonants. As smoke rose in the circle, however, I began to worry – the reddish color of the smoke didn't blend properly with the lighting. I couldn't remember if that was important in Thelmastii workings. I started frantically leafing through the text, hoping to find annotations that would let me know what he was trying to do. Perry laughed at me, though, saying that everything was under control.

The smoke didn't exactly clear, but it did coalesce into a ball. When it finished, the inhabiting spirit hovered for a moment and said, if I remember my Thelmastii correctly, "Which side of the octagon knows not the face?"

I didn't know that riddle. It sounded like a metaphysical take on Kelk's Third Law of Magical Structure, but it wasn't exactly my field. Unfortunately, Perry didn't know it either. He started to stall for time, and then realized he had to answer immediately. The trick with Thelmastii spirits is that they are bound not by power, but by knowledge. Hesitation at a moment like that is an admission of ignorance. Perry panicked, and guessed.

I awoke around dawn, with the aching combination of bruising and failure that I had all but forgotten from my days as an apprentice. I surveyed the shambled room: bookcases overturned, shelves collapsed, notes and equipment scattered, and doors blasted off of their hinges.

I was still looking over the damage when Perry woke up. I think he came out of it worse than I did, showing that magic has some sense of justice at least. "Where is it?" he rasped.

"Well, it's not bound, that's for sure."

"Not quite what I had in mind," he said with a chuckle, "but it was a show."

"I guess it was at that."

"Will you help me find it?"

"I better. Otherwise you're likely to do something stupid like summon another one to see if it leads you to the first."

We laughed at that for a moment before Perry said, "Do you think that would work?"

***

WE HAD TO PREPARE BEFORE TRACKING DOWN THE SPIRIT, SO CLEANING his lab was the first order of business. I was righting and organizing a tumbled shelf of books when I asked, "What was that thing anyway?"

"Thelmastii," he said as he scooped ash and dead coals back into the brazier. Good thing that the ritual didn't require its use or the house might have burned down around us.

"Focus, Perry."

"Oh, right. It's a spirit of visions, supposed to excel at illusions and hallucinations."

"That would have rounded out the evening well. Shame the binding didn't take." I looked again at the shelf I was organizing. A vision spirit. . . . "Do you have a plain white candle?"

"Sure, in the workbench, third drawer down."

I found three in that drawer, mixed in haphazardly with other solid colors. I took a carving tool and inscribed the proper runes on one. Normally I would have foregone the candle, but my head still throbbed. Perry stopped cleaning up ash and watched as I chanted over the unlit wick.

The candle flamed blue-green for a moment and vaporized in a puff of smoke. Perry's laboratory was now neat and clean, or at least as tidy as one might expect following a night of drinking, nostalgia, and Crossed Purposes. Here were empty glasses and bottles, there the remains of our food, and the game board sat ready for the next contest.

"Kornah's iron hand," said Perry. "It was all an illusion." He stood, then doubled over clutching his back. "Perhaps not all of it." He straightened more slowly, and began poking and prodding at his bruises.

"So was that its worst or a warning?"

"Tough to say, but we should be fine as long as it's just the one."

"You only summoned one, right?"

"Of course! But without a binding, after it has time to attune itself to our world it can bring through others to keep it company. That won't be for about a day though. In fact, they say the Thelmasts fell because an apprentice. . ."

"Hey, we should get moving."

A pretender to the sage's art
Shall fail in body, mind and heart.

"One more word out of you and I'll smash you into kindling!" roared Perry at the chalkboard. It had been having a great deal of fun at our expense, mocking us in three languages so far: Florese, Chaldish, and that last bit was Aarkadian.

"Focus, Perry" I said, stepping between them. "You're the one who's been studying Thelmastii magic lately. Where is one of their vision spirits likely to go?"

"They feed on deception and misdirection, so maybe the docks? The stories told by sailors and criminals would be a feast."

"Maybe the magistrate. People always lie in court."

"Not the magistrate's court! The Count's court! Lying is a noble's favorite pastime!"

We grabbed a few things we might need on the hunt and started puzzling through the riddle. I was convinced that the answer was the "inside" because the inside cannot face anything.

Perry insisted that the answer was the "outside" because octagons are used for protection and binding. Thus, as containers, the outside would never be "faced." We had not settled on an answer when we boarded Perry's coach and flew through the streets. We argued about it the whole way to Hawk's Perch, the keep of Count Erich of Glabarth, the Son of the Hawk.

The guards admitted us without challenge because we were both known to have the Count's patronage. We were just starting after our quarry when a page spotted us.

"Welcome, good sirs. Shall I announce you to His Excellency? His court schedule is full for the day, but I am certain he would make time for you both."

"That won't be necessary," said Perry.

"We're just here to check the details on some of our work," I said. "It wouldn't do to have any of His Excellency's lights dim or scenes lose cohesion."

"Can that happen?" The surprise in the page's voice gave me a swell of pride.

"Not usually, but there's been a fluctuation in the local aetheric continuum which can cause instability along the fifth and sixth lines of power among. . . . But I don't want to trouble you with the details.

Suffice to say that environmental conditions have necessitated a verification that all is in order."

"Of course, sir. I won't take up any more of your time, sirs." He scuttled off and Perry smirked at me. "Aetheric continuum?"

"Well, in Velstadt they teach that...."

"Aetheric continuum?"

"Well I didn't hear you offer anything better."

He chuckled softly in response and we began our search.

ONE OF THE FIRST TOOLS AN APPRENTICE LEARNS TO MAKE IS HIS monocle. It's a sort of jeweler's eye for wizards; it sharpens our perception, helping us analyze spells and notice magical discrepancies in the world around us. Using our monocles to find the vision spirit meant wearing them constantly.

It's not that the monocles are dangerous; it's more that they are uncomfortable to use for extended periods of time or for examining a large area. Imagine trying to read small, yellow letters on a burning log. Compared to that, what we were doing that day was like reading a novel written on a burning wall. A few hours of this and our eyes were strained and our heads pounding beyond even last night's bruising.

We were examining a hallway near the reception room, set with alcoves for private meetings and a series of illusions just loud enough to prevent casual eavesdropping, when in strolled Lady Geraldine, fourth child and second daughter of His Excellency. She was young enough to be unmarried, old enough to be beautiful, and savvy enough to know what this combination meant in a Count's daughter.

"Admiring your work, good wizards?"

Perry couldn't find his tongue quickly enough – he might have had an easier time if he managed to close his jaw – so I had to answer for us both. "I'm afraid not, my lady. Atmospheric conditions have made it necessary for us to ensure that our spells here have not suffered from a sort of... interference."

She posed in thoughtful consideration of my illusory scene. Always at work, I made a rapid mental sketch of her in case a future commission called for a similar image. Finally, she spoke, "It appears as it always does, at least to my unlearned eye.

"This one has always been a favorite of mine. The flow of the waterfall is almost musical, even if my father only wanted it as cover for quiet conversations. I also like the arrangement of the shrubs and flowers, and the hare and doe that appear from time to time. You really are quite an artist."

"Thank you, my lady. My lady is most kind." As I stood from my bow, I noticed a small inconsistency in the air behind her that had nothing to do with my illusion. Just a little distortion, but my monocle-induced headache vanished.

Perry saw it a moment after I did. His tongue still eluded him, but he reached toward me to draw my attention while keeping his eyes on the distortion.

"Such troubled faces," said Lady Geraldine with a puzzled frown. "My nurse used to say that when a wizard looks troubled, he sees the calm before the storm. Tell me, is a storm approaching?" As she spoke, she glanced about surreptitiously, trying to spot the object of our attention.

"Well, my lady, that depends. Is my lady accustomed to being followed by a spirit?"

"Oh, this old thing?" she asked, waving one hand dismissively. Her eyes had widened, just a flicker, but it passed as though it had never been. "It's been a minor irritation for some days now. I've been meaning to have a priest banish it back to the netherworld, only I haven't been able to spare the time." I swear I thought I saw the distortion grow bigger as she spoke. "Why? Could you banish it as well as a priest?"

"For some days, you said?" choked Perry.

"A few days or a week I should think." She considered for a moment. She seemed to enjoy tilting her head at just the right angle to drape her dark, luxurious hair down her neck. "A week. I recall now that I first noticed it after Father met with the Barons this past Secondday."

Perry looked confused, but my only question was whether she was lying or being tricked by the spirit. I gambled on the former. "We would be only too happy to banish it for my lady, if only. . . ." I was interrupted by the staccato sound of Perry's rapid chant. He threw a handful's worth of a reflective powder made from ground sand and obsidian before I could stop him.

Both the distortion and Lady Geraldine were gone and I felt like a novice. Illusions had always been my specialty, but I had missed this one completely. Fortunately Perry had not only spotted it, but also thrown and activated some Vinfin Dust, a Thelmastii concoction that stuns a spirit and disrupts its magic. It would only buy us a moment, but I recovered quickly enough to chant the Formula of Importunement while Perry whipped together a binding circle of light.

The spirit came to itself about the time we finished, testing the limits of the circle with tendrils while regarding us with smoky eyes. When it found no flaws in the holding spell it swelled slightly and said in its hollow voice, "The third path of necromancy opens only to those who possess two virtues and one failing. Name them."

King Osric III outlawed necromancy some 350 years ago. We never had a chance at this one.

Suddenly night had fallen and my legs and back were stiff, cramped and exhausted. Perry was in a similar state, and when the guards approached we were trying to walk some feeling back into them.

"I would have your names and business, sirs," said their leader, the captain himself. The other four guards fanned out behind him, spears held ready but not yet menacing us. We gave our names and he relaxed a bit, but our business, examining our spells, troubled him. "I'm sorry, sirs, but His Excellency has given leave for no overnight visitors. If your business requires it, I am certain you will be welcomed back in the morning, but for now I must ask that we escort you to your carriage."

"What time is it, Captain?"

"The clock should strike midnight soon, sir."

"Of course, of course," I said, trying to cover my astonishment. "I apologize for our remaining so late, but when we are working, we poor wizards tend to forget such things as food, sleep and the passage of time." Our empty stomachs rumbled in support. "Of course we'll accompany you."

Neither Perry nor I spoke again until we were back on the road and safely alone. "The book didn't say anything about the riddle changing with each attempt at binding. And necromancy? Isn't that cheating?"

"I don't think it worries about the laws of the land. What tipped you off about Lady Geraldine?"

"With all due respect to Lady Geraldine, no one is that beautiful. I can't believe it made time just . . . evaporate on us. Can you do that?"

"No . . . no, I can't. Would you stop the carriage a moment?" The carriage slowed to a halt and Perry looked at me expectantly. I climbed down to the street and he followed. We were only a turn or two from Perry's house, and the neighborhood was full of good tradesmen and women who were likely already in bed. The street was empty under the clear sky. The moon was almost half-full, and the star positions were right. A breeze blew gently, as one might expect in late spring, and smelled slightly of the flower shop on the corner. Everything seemed in order, but I couldn't be sure. What if we were still in the hallway?

I pulled a white candle from a pouch at my belt, this one already inscribed with the proper runes. When the candle vanished in a puff of smoke at the end of my spell, nothing had changed.

"Not an illusion then?" asked Perry.

I shook my head.

"At least we know it didn't stay at Hawk's Perch." At my surprised look he continued, "It would get bored while everyone is sleeping. The spirit isn't mindless. Once it's done feeding, it will seek entertainment until it needs rest. And before you ask, no, I don't know how it rests or what a likely location is. . . ."

I had stopped listening by then. It wanted amusement. I grabbed a handful of my Vinfin Dust, spun in a circle and scattered it widely while incanting the activation. In the middle of the dust cloud was the shape we were looking for.

"Ha!" cried Perry, before launching into his spell to create a binding circle of pure light around it while I repeated the Formula of Importunement. As soon as it finished testing the circle, it regarded us with its alien gaze. Finally it spoke, in a voice as misty as its body. "What curse did the Aarkadi visit upon those who would steal their knowledge?"

Something gnawed at the back of my mind, but Perry beat me to it.

> *A pretender to the sage's art*
> *Shall fail in body, mind and heart.*

I noted that his Aarkadian had improved recently, probably the chalkboard's influence. Then I remembered why it sounded familiar – and familiar was the right word.

While I was getting it straight in my head Perry was speaking rapidly in Thelmastii:

> Summoned forth by ancient rite,
> Bound here by my wisdom.
> Sixteen days I claim by right,
> And then you must go home.

The spirit responded in haunting tones:

> Your magic strong, your wisdom true,
> I will keep your bargain.
> Ten days and six I grant to you,
> Then home I go again.

Perry pulled out an intricately carved bottle and extended it into the circle. The tiny container looked far too small to contain the smoke-filled spirit flowing into it, but somehow the deed was done. Once the engraved stopper was in place Perry released the circle and presented the bottle to me with a flourish and a broad grin.

"What's this?" I asked.

"Look, you helped me rework the business and presentation side of my magic to appeal to the upper classes. If it weren't for you, I'd still be lighting warehouses and making pallet movers.

"I thought a Thelmastii vision spirit might have a trick or two that could help you the way you helped me. It's only for sixteen days, but that's a standard Thelmastii deal. Something to do with how they tracked time, I think."

"Thank you, Perry."

"You are quite welcome, my friend. Now, if you will return to my coach, I believe a celebratory drink is in order."

"And a meal."

We laughed at ourselves the rest of the way to Perry's. As we entered his workshop, the professional surrounding brought me back to the spirit bottle in my hand. "I wonder if the spirit can teach me that time trick. I can think of several applications for it and if I can tweak the parameters . . ."

"Look at that," said Perry, pointing at the chalkboard. It was as blank and clean as though it had been washed. "There's no insult."

I was just starting in on what little I knew about the theory of temporal illusions and the areas I hoped the spirit could clarify when two words appeared on the chalkboard in our own native language: "The fourth."

"What?" said Perry.

For once, the chalkboard elaborated. "The fourth side of the octagon knows not the face. It's a trick question based on Kelk's Third Law of Magical Structure. The fourth side is always down when the octagon is vertical, and behind the wizard when the octagon is horizontal. Thus, the fourth side is never faced by the wizard and therefore 'knows not the face.'"

"You could have said something sooner."

"You bound me into a chalkboard!"

"Why tell me now?"

"If you can bind a Thelmastii spirit, I'd say you're at least worth talking to."

We drank to that.

NOT THAT KIND OF
WIZARD

Sixth of Remembrance, Forty-fifth Year of King Morann

They did not execute me. Rather, they promoted me, which may be worse.

I had been recalled to the palace in the company of deserters and spies, a three day trip I would not care to repeat under the best of circumstances, much less under guard at a pace that nearly killed four horses. I could think of no crime, save perhaps cowardice in the face of the enemy. But every man is a coward in the face of certain death, whether he acts on his fear or not. Still, His Majesty is not called "the Sword of Fury" for his even temperament.

Yet when I stood before the throne under the hot-poker gaze of His Majesty, awaiting His call for the executioner, He asked me questions. "Why did you lead your hand off of the trail?"

"Sire, I heard enemy troops approaching. I was afraid."

"Were they your hand to lead?"

"No, Sire. But we were moving to a set position through land we were supposed to control. There should have been no opposition. The enemy outnumbered us. If we met them head on, we would have died and no one would have reported the lapse in our picket before the Quartati brought more troops through."

"What did your commander think?"

"Our thumb wanted to lead us around the Quartati and make our rendezvous on schedule, report then."

"Instead you took six men and killed how many Quartati?"

"Fifty, but only because I knew of an ambush point invisible from the Quartat approach. Easy kills for good crossbowmen. We took out the better part of an arm before they got word back that their plan had been compromised."

The king smiled then, and though I suspected He meant it as a friendly gesture, my guts turned as cold and watery as they had in the face of those Quartati. He gave me the "good" news and clapped my back. Shock reverberated through my body like a death knell.

I'm a thumb now, and tomorrow I meet the rest of my hand for a special assignment that I'm sure brings us back to the front, maybe even behind enemy lines.

I doubt I'll be sleeping tonight.

SEVENTH OF REMEMBRANCE, FORTY-FIFTH YEAR OF KING MORANN

Already on the road. I've got a small hand, three men, and a task that sounds simple: escort a wizard behind enemy lines. Officially I haven't been told that Skelly is a wizard, but he is a bald little old man in a brown robe, with a walking stick and clean-shaven face. He is either a wizard or a priest, and I doubt there's much strategic advantage to escorting a priest behind enemy lines.

He has the charm of a priest though. Skelly has this little smile always hovering around his lips and hiding behind his eyes. He speaks gently, he moves gently, he even eats gently. He ate less of our supper than I did, and I can barely keep food down right now.

Cordon ate enough for the three of us though. He wears on his back the biggest sword I've ever seen, which sounds fair because Cordon is the biggest man I've ever seen. Either that, or the king had someone shave a bear and strap a sword to its back. If the time comes for a ranged fight, I don't know if Cordon will fire his crossbow or throw it.

Dirk looks like his namesake, slight and quick, with a slender sword and a half-dozen daggers that I can see. He brought down our dinner with a crossbow bolt through the eye of a ptarmigan and cleaned it faster than I can clean my sword. Good thing, too. As much as Cordon eats, I worry about having enough food for the return trip. Assuming there will be a return trip.

Lunn is the oldest of us, apart from Skelly. I think his scabbard is older than I am. Dirk looks at Lunn as though he expects him to fall over any moment, which just means he has yet to hear the stories. They say Lunn stood as champion for three different earls on the same day and won every duel. Lunn once turned a route into a victory by holding a pass against a hundred Yollish regulars. They say a lot more too, but when I asked Lunn how many of the stories were true he only said, "Enough." I can't understand why I'm thumb and he's just a finger.

Anyway, a small hand but a good one. Too bad this is a suicide mission.

Eighth of Remembrance, Forty-fifth Year of King Morann

We're already behind schedule.

Baron Carmigen, who detailed the route we are to follow, made clear to me that we were to cut directly across the chaparral to where it meets the river, then down to the woods. The first few hundred yards off of the road went up a steep slope, but hardened soldiers know that means having the afternoon sun on our backs instead of in our eyes. Simple enough path for a competent hand.

Apparently not so simple for an old "wizard." Skelly's pace may not disturb the ground, but I could have rolled up that slope faster than he hiked it. We had to stop every fifty yards to keep the old fool from falling too far behind. Cordon started snapping twigs off of limbs, tossing them into the underbrush. Dirk leaned against a pine tree, one foot on the bark, and alternated between drumming his fingers and checking and rechecking his daggers. Eight in all, unless there were a few he didn't check. Lunn stood still as a rock while we waited. I'm not sure he even blinked.

The second time Skelly caught up to us, his lips relaxed into a smile and he said, "At my age, hills don't flatten out as quickly as they used to." Then he chuckled, as though he meant that to amuse us.

"Can't you just fly to the top?" said Dirk.

"I'm not that kind of wizard."

"Could you become a bird?" I tried to take control before Cordon picked the old man up and carried him. The Baron had insisted that we treat Skelly with respect, and I had no intention of managing to survive this mission only to get a worse one on a charge of insolence. "Perhaps a cougar?"

Skelly shook his head and kept walking. I made my hand slow their pace to match his.

If I read the sunset right, we finished the day's hike a good three hours short of where we were supposed to be.

At least the old bastard can come down a slope faster than he can ascend one.

Ninth of Remembrance, Forty-fifth Year of King Morann

Made it into the woods today. I don't think we've fallen any further behind.

Ate well tonight. Lunn brought down a huge turkey. Cordon and Dirk had no end of sport with the accomplishment, since Lunn had stepped into the trees to relieve himself.

The roast turkey seems to have improved the mood of the hand after yesterday's impatience. The prospect of leftovers encourages watch rotation, so long as Cordon takes last watch.

Skelly sits oblivious, perpetually one moment away from a broad smile. I'm not even sure he sleeps. He just sits there all night by the fire, legs folded, back straight. Perhaps he isn't a wizard at all. Perhaps he's the simple uncle of a Quartat commander, and we're his escort to the prisoner exchange.

Tenth of Remembrance, Forty-fifth Year of King Morann

I'm worried about how well we control these lands. I've seen no sign of Quartati, and I haven't asked my men yet because I don't want to set them on edge. Skelly does that well enough without my adding to the mess. I wonder though, whether the peasantry might grow tired of His Highness, or perhaps of this war, which has endured past the decade mark.

According to the Baron's timetable, by noon we should have found a footbridge across Hermione's River of Tears. Even accounting for our lost time, we should have found it by mid-afternoon. About an hour before dusk we had to give up the search and accept that someone had sunk it.

Fast and wide as the tears of that old queen were said to be after the loss of her husband and eldest son in the same battle, that river was too rough for us to swim across. Well, perhaps Lunn would have made it, but the rest of us could not have, and certainly not Skelly.

We needed to fell a tree tall enough to get us across. I asked Skelly if he could accomplish this with his "magic."

Skelly smiled, shook his head, and said, "I'm not that kind of wizard." He then stood, waiting, confident that we would get him across that river.

Fortunately Lunn and Cordon carried hatchets in their packs. The sun was well down by the time we got across that river, Dirk half-carrying Skelly under the pretense of guiding the old fool's steps.

No time to hunt. Cold camp and rations tonight. I can tell from the mutters of Cordon and Dirk that their impatience with Skelly grows faster even than mine. Only Lunn guards his temper within himself. If Skelly hears the grumbling, it does not appear to dull his humor. More the fool he.

That sunken bridge worries me. I had thought of the watch rotation as a formality, a means of keeping discipline in a new hand and ensuring that the men had work. Now I fear that we might need one ready blade at all times.

Perhaps I was mistaken. Perhaps I never was promoted, and this assignment is my form of execution.

ELEVENTH OF REMEMBRANCE, FORTY-FIFTH YEAR OF KING MORANN

This assignment has me jumping at shadows. I kept myself on high alert all day, but saw no signs of pursuit, no traps from peasant hunters out to open the borders to Quartat invaders. Perhaps the winter's rain was greater than most and washed the bridge out. The Baron had warned me it was never more than a simple footbridge, rough wood and minimal effort rather than fancy masonry. Perhaps local hunters sink the bridge from time to time to guard their chosen territories.

In any event, the day's travel went well. I roused the men early, and since I knew I had no hope of pushing Skelly's pace, I skipped the first rest period to see how he handled it.

Skelly didn't notice!

The old fool kept walking as though he could continue all day without rest, so that's what I made him do. That the men had to march without a break was made easier by Skelly's temperament – if he could handle this pace without complaint, then how could fit young men like them do any less?

We lunched on the march, and by the time I called the halt, we must have made up a quarter day's time. If we can do that again tomorrow we should be back on schedule.

Dinner was another ptarmigan, this time with apples we came by during the march. The smell of roasting apples still reminds me of hunting with Parlan. I hope he's treating Clarissa well and raising my nephews right.

Tomorrow will be our last day in friendly territory. Soon the border and the battle lines, and getting the old fool wherever exactly it is he's supposed to go. I'm still irritated that the Baron only said, "Once you get into Quartat territory, Skelly will guide you the rest of the way."

May Janna the Merciful grant that I dream tonight of roasting apples with my brother, not of battles and war.

Twelfth of Remembrance, Forty-fifth Year of King Morann

Dirk is dead.

It was just after noon. I'd started the day's march early again and pressed us through breaks to make up time. I pushed too hard. Our attention must have flagged. Anyway, Cordon and Dirk were arguing about the best way to prepare rabbit when Skelly said, "Duck."

Lunn and I hit the ground as fast as the old man, but a quarrel struck Dirk in the side of the throat, spraying Cordon with blood. I tracked the quarrel's flight with my eyes and saw a group of farmhands playing soldier. Six of them with light crossbows. No swords, no armor, and none of them old enough to have a man's voice or strength. But they had their hair cut to a soldier's length, and they wore red rags tied at their left shoulders, one with a black mark, as though they considered themselves a hand with a thumb.

One of those crossbows was empty, and the boy who held it looked sick.

I shouted orders in our battle tongue. *"Cordon, retreat with objective. Lunn, cover fire."*

Cordon grabbed the old man and carried him out of the field of fire. Lunn shot Dirk's killer. I shot the would-be thumb. The others broke and ran, yelling, "Soldiers! Soldiers!"

Lunn was on his feet before I could blink, pulling me to mine. We found Cordon and ran off route for twenty minutes, then turned parallel and maintained a quick hike. Lunn guided, Cordon carried Skelly, and I provided cover. I kept us at that for half our remaining sun before I called a rest break.

As far as I could tell, Skelly never noticed that Cordon was carrying him. His face held that same absent humor, though he did shake his head from time to time. Now I wish I'd just had Cordon carry him up that damned slope. We could have been on schedule and Dirk might still be alive.

During the break, Cordon asked the question that was on my mind, "Why did a bunch of farmhands try to kill us?"

"Sons of Quartat," said Lunn, like it was a title and not a fact of birth. So I repeated it like a question. He elaborated. "Border's been close to here for a long time. Bastards grow up on both sides. Some feel loyalty to absent fathers, act like they live in occupied territory." He shrugged. "Some take up arms."

"Will they pursue?" I asked.

"Probably not. Some lay ambushes, but most like the idea of battle better than the reality." He shook his head. "None of them would risk a straight fight."

"Think they have contact with the Quartati proper?"

"Safer to assume they do."

I called an early night, though long watch rotations meant less sleep for everyone except Skelly. Can't risk returning to our designated route until we've crossed into enemy territory so we'll have to push harder to stay on schedule.

I could kill that Baron for not telling me about the Sons of Quartat in my briefing. I'd ask Skelly if he had any way of detecting them or stopping them or maybe making us invisible, but I'm sure he's not that kind of wizard.

I'm sorry, Dirk.

THIRTEENTH OF REMEMBRANCE, FORTY-FIFTH YEAR OF KING MORANN

Today was a disaster. I'm no thumb, just a finger who got lucky. Made a decision that worked out, knew a little terrain better than my enemy. Morann was a fool to put men's lives in my slippery grasp.

We're down to me and Skelly. Not that I believe Lunn is dead. I won't believe that until I see his corpse. But I have seen Cordon's.

I woke everyone early again and had us hiking before dawn. Even Skelly kept a brisker pace. I started to believe that the old fool finally understood that we're in danger. If he didn't then, he must now.

I wanted to bring us back to the river, use it to create a break in our tracks, but could not risk the exposure. Instead I brought us further East, off course, hoping to disguise our true route. I led today, with Cordon in the middle to guard Skelly and Lunn covering our rear. By noon Lunn was certain we were not followed. I interpreted that to mean that the farmhands were done playing soldier and started angling my hand back to its designated route.

I should have considered that one need not be a soldier to deliver a message.

We reached the Quartat border by mid-afternoon. That meant we had been in contested territory for an hour or so. If we had crossed the river and traveled another hour or so West, we would have reached the fighting. In the woods where we were, I would not have known that we had reached the border if Lunn had not stopped us to point out a small cairn three hundred paces East. Apparently such cairns are placed every thousand paces to mark the boundary after a treaty is drawn up. In practice they mainly serve to warn hunters when they cross into a different set of laws.

If I survive this mission, I'm either going to kill Baron Carmigen or petition to have a formal training process for thumbs, to eliminate gaping knowledge gaps like mine.

Perhaps I'll do both.

We had taken perhaps fifty steps past the border when Skelly said, "Don't step there."

I looked back and saw Cordon get yanked up into the trees by a rope snare around his ankle. I dove and tackled Skelly to the ground just as the ambush sprung. Arrows filled the air, one piercing my left arm. It felt like someone the size of Cordon had jumped on my forearm in boots and full armor.

Lunn screamed, "The mission," in battle tongue. Arrow in his shoulder, he charged the ambush with his sword held high. Yet he moved so slowly. I could only marvel at how slow he ran, the loud roar of a waterfall in my ears, the dull awareness of a shaft of wood sticking out of my arm, the three others in the chest of the dangling Cordon, his tongue lolling out.

Skelly touched my face and said, "We must flee."

Lunn moved fast now, his sword whirling and a thrown dagger preceding his charge. The waterfall roar dimmed to a rapid thump. I pulled Skelly to his feet and we ran.

Damn Skelly. Damn my mission. My last living finger charged our ambush without me. I should have been there with him. Together we might have made it out alive. Not that Skelly would have been any help. So Lunn and I might have made it, but Skelly and the mission would have died.

I know that's what Lunn was telling me. Get Skelly out of there and finish the mission. I hate it.

I don't know how long I ran, carrying Skelly, before I collapsed. I don't know how long I was out before I came to, but we had an hour before sunset. The arrow was gone from my arm, a strip of clean cloth in its place. Skelly sat next to me, legs folded under him the same way he passed every night.

"You know healing magic?"

"I'm not that kind of wizard. This was a simple charm to improve the poultice. The pain will return soon, and the poultice must be replaced at dawn."

"Well ... thank you."

Skelly nodded. I think he would have been content to sit there until the forest grew over him, but I wanted to put more space between us and those Quartati. We pushed on until darkness made further travel unsafe. Skelly led the way now, certain of the territory and direction. He seemed so comfortable that before I slept that night I had to ask, "Are you from Quartat?"

"If I were it would not help us. My youth was long, long ago."

After an answer like that, I didn't see any point in further questions.

Dirk, and now Cordon, and maybe even Lunn. I hope this old man is worth their deaths.

Cordon carried the extra food, so Skelly and I will have to share rations until we cross the border again. Assuming we do.

And he was right about the pain coming back. I hope I can sleep at least a little tonight.

FOURTEENTH OF REMEMBRANCE, FORTY-FIFTH YEAR OF KING MORANN

I now believe every story I've ever heard about Lunn. Even the one about the six barmaids, because I cannot bring myself to doubt the man's stamina.

Lunn caught up with us while we broke for lunch. Alone, wounded, in enemy territory. Despite our lead and that Skelly alone knew our destination. *Lunn caught up with us.*

I didn't hear him approach. Skelly looked up from a bite of dried beef and smiled. I followed his gaze and there was Lunn. He dropped Cordon's sack of extra food between us, sat, and tore into his own rations.

"I can't believe you escaped," I said.

"Not escaped. Won. There were only six, and that was a poor excuse for an ambush. Must have been rushed."

That was all Lunn had to say about it. Despite Skelly's poultices, I think the wound in my forearm bothers me more than the arrow I saw pierce Lunn's shoulder. If he took any other wounds in that ambush, I can't tell.

I worry about our direction. We travel almost due East, with occasional corrections North and South. Lunn suspects that we're avoiding patrols, but how could Skelly know current patrol routes? Even Lunn had to admit that he has not seen nor heard any sign of the enemy.

We sleep tonight huddled in a small grove of trees on the side of a hill. Skelly says that tomorrow he will show us why we brought him here.

Soon it will be over one way or the other.

FIFTEENTH OF REMEMBRANCE, FORTY-FIFTH YEAR OF KING MORANN

I wish His Majesty had executed me. What I saw today...

We rose at dawn, and Skelly changed my poultice. His gentle smile and touch. I wish he'd been a healer.

We spent the day ascending. One hill, a second, and finally to a plateau. Skelly kept a better pace now, his step almost eager. Could he have been looking forward to this?

We did not stop for rest, ate rations as we hiked. By mid-afternoon we stood high on that plateau, and from there we could see the main body of the Quartat forces, tens of thousands strong, arrayed in the valley below. Command flags and tents, not only soldiers, the cream of Quartat nobility arrayed before us.

Skelly raised his hands, and my stomach began to sour. He chanted words that grated against my ears, stilled the air around us. No birds, not even a gopher stirred as his chant continued. The sun above us flared hotter, brighter, blinding, burning...

I cringed behind my arm, could barely see between squeezing eyelids as *the sun fell from the sky*. The sun itself dropped into that valley and consumed it in a flash.

And then it was gone. Back up in the sky as though nothing had happened. Except that no life stirred in the valley below. Birds, horses, sheep, cattle, grass, trees, rocks, and countless Quartati reduced to ash, burned too fine for even the smell to escape.

I fell to my knees and retched, tears hot on my cheeks, unburned despite my expectations.

Skelly laughed. Cruel and triumphant the sound twisted in my ears, turned my head to look at him. He stood, arms outstretched, glorying in his work. I fell into my own puddle of sick, legs pumping, desperate to push me away from his mad eyes, uncaring that I risked going over the edge.

With a single movement, Lunn drew his sword and beheaded Skelly. Blood flew higher than I expected from such a little man. Skelly's head bounced over the ledge and plummeted to land among his handiwork. With an impatient sigh, a blood-spattered Lunn reached down and grabbed one of my still-pumping legs, pulled me to safety.

"We better clean up," said Lunn.

I couldn't speak. Just stared at him.

"Seen it before," he said. "Spell changes a wizard. Have to kill them during the afterglow or else." He looked at the body. "Shame. Liked the old bastard."

I threw down my sword and ran. I didn't care where at first, just away from that valley, from the war, from all of it. I ran until I had to walk, walked until I had to crawl, then I climbed the nearest tree. Tonight I'll sleep strapped to a branch. If I get the memory of that spell out of my head long enough to sleep.

Better Morann had executed me.

HALF A POUND OF MAGIC

They found Xorek in the temple of Suuni the Passionate. By his reputation he should have been sacking that temple, night black plates of armor on his back, twirling blade Shadowcarver in one hand, and a chorus of demons slaying and razing all about him.

But the man they saw knelt as though in prayer before the golden statue of The Most Beautiful. In place of a sword he wore a long dagger with a hilt carved from bone. In place of midnight plates he bore worn dusky leathers. But he was of a height, his hands scarred, his shoulders broad, and his hair red as old blood.

He looked dangerous, but not like a man who needed five of them. Still, they knew that no warrior grew his reputation without spilling lives.

The main room of the temple would work to their advantage: intimate, hushed. Subdued candlelight. Several doors along the walls to escape, but none near their target, and each beside its own sensuous marble statue. Easily blocked off. Rich rugs and tapestries would mute their boots on the marble floor. Sweet, honeyed incense already excited their blood.

No doubt the aroma was intended to inspire lust. But fire in the veins swung swords as well.

And all five of them had swords, and padded chain armor.

Two soft steps through the door they were met by a priestess of surpassing beauty, clad only in a wispy robe that did more to enhance than cover her. She stepped in front of them and placed one finger before her dark lips, managing to suggest as well as hush with the gesture. Her chocolate eyes smiled.

"This is not a place of violence," she said, voice husky. "Come, leave your scores outside and let us find you a way to worship the goddess as she prefers."

Their leader shook his head and pointed an angry finger at Xorek, the passion in his own mind fixed on his task.

"Very well, but I warn you. Men who raise weapons in the temple of Suuni often find weapons are the only things they can raise."

The leader stepped past the priestess. His men followed, though he noticed their reluctance. But perhaps they did not fear the curse.

Or the kneeling man. Perhaps they had not yet prepared themselves to kill, as their leader had.

With slow, quiet steps the five fanned out behind their target. Cutting off escape.

At the leader's nod, they drew their swords.

"You should heed the priestess," said Xorek, still kneeling before the statue. "She Whose Passions Rule Us All will not forgive an insult for the price of a donation."

The leader could still see hesitation in his men. Hilts gripped by uncertain hands. Concerned backs straightened from ready poses. He knew they feared the rumors of Xorek's magic.

But the leader was ready. He did not see Xorek before him, neither man nor reputation. He saw only his target: Xorek's exposed neck.

The leader lunged for the quick kill.

But the leader did not realize how brightly polished that statue was. He did not know that Xorek had watched their approach. Seen how they had arrayed themselves. Waited for the leader to prepare his thrust.

So when Xorek rolled to his right away from the blade, the leader was shocked to see his thrust miss. His men saw the perfect timing of the dodge and feared that Xorek's magic warned him of the strike.

Two dropped their swords and ran, overwhelmed by the threat of Xorek's magic and Suuni's curse. The other two stared slack-jawed, swords pointed down and useless, if only for a moment.

But a moment was enough.

The leader overbalanced with his lunge. Staggered forward a step to recover. Xorek sprang, carried him to the floor face down.

The leader struggled to breathe around deep carpeting, pressed down by the weight of his target. His sword hand useless under a sharp knee.

A sharper blade dented his throat.

"Drop your swords," said Xorek, as though bored by the whole encounter.

The leader heard twin muffled thumps.

"You have cut the livery from your coats," said Xorek, "but your clothes aren't weather-worn enough for you to have ridden far. So you must have come from that fat slob Ursa."

"*Graefe* Ursa," growled the leader.

"That settles that then," said Xorek, a watchful eye on the two remaining swordsmen, though they showed no signs of going for their discarded weapons.

"I suppose I really should kill you," he continued, baritone voice conversational. "You seem the type to take failure personally and try again. And honestly, I think most men would be happier dying than living with what Suuni will do to you."

Xorek smiled as the standing warriors paled further.

"Oh, yes. The high priestess made no idle threat. I suggest you speak to her about atonement." Xorek's voice grew hard. "But not today. Today you leave your swords and run back to your master with the tale of your failure. And tell him that I will thank him personally for your visit. Sooner than he expects."

With that Xorek stood, his foot on the leader's sword to discourage a change of heart. The remaining three would-be assassins rushed from the temple.

As the high priestess approached Xorek, he said, "I trust you can sell these swords and make good use of the money?"

"Of course," she said, mystery in her smile.

Xorek held up his bone-handled long knife, before slipping it back into its sheath. "Will I be forgiven for drawing this weapon to defend myself?"

"You spilled no blood, nor tried to."

The clench of Xorek's jaw suggested that he had not realized how close he came to sharing the assassins' curse.

"Still," said the priestess, her voice husky, "better safe than sorry." She reached out a hand. "Will you come worship with me?"

"My belovéd may be trapped, but I will touch no other woman in her place."

"Even better," said the priestess. "For Suuni smiles on the passion that inspires such devotion. May you free her soon."

A door along the right-hand wall opened and out came a slender man with curly black hair and a rakish grin. Like Xorek he dressed in dusky leathers, though he wore a long, thin blade at his hip and concealed more daggers about his person than any man had a right to expect. As he approached, the high priestess stepped through the open door and closed it behind her.

"Finished at last, Karvan?" said Xorek.

"Worshiping properly takes time," said Karvan. "And repetition." He stretched his arms above his head. "Did your prayers bring you inspiration?"

"After a fashion. A hand came to kill me."

Karvan made a show of looking his friend up and down.

"I'd say they failed."

"It wasn't a serious attempt. Only one hardened killer." Xorek shook his head. "And had they been serious they would have waited outside with bows."

Karvan raised an expressive eyebrow.

"Very well," said Xorek with a sigh.

Xorek rubbed his left arm three times while uttering harsh syllables in the language of lost Xechaglossa, calling forth a dark orange, scaled imp from the woven leather bracelet Xorek wore beneath his armor.

The imp, two hand spans tall with eyes like a hawk and a pointed chin adorned with a feathery beard, crossed its arms and scowled.

"Here? You call me here? Passion surges from the very stones! I could be crushed."

"Go forth for me, Oolniph, and search the trees, the air, the ground, the rocks. If enemies lie in wait, I must know."

The imp scowled, but said nothing. It vanished, leaving behind only a sideways orange stain that faded slowly from the air.

"Who sent the hand?" asked Karvan.

"Ursa, of course. He controls the jalemroot. No doubt he knows by now that we seek it. And how much we need."

Jalemroot grew in sparse quantities when it grew at all, and only in mines exhausted of their gold. And Ursa exhausted every vein he tapped.

"Then why not send real killers?"

Oolniph reformed in the air before Xorek's face and said, "Unless the bears and wolves seek your blood, no threats await you within a quarter-day's ride."

The imp vanished before Xorek could ask about the hand, but he could not deny that Oolniph had completed its task, its second of three for the day.

Karvan waited for his answer.

"Ursa may be a fat slob, but he's shrewd enough. He knew even a good hand would fail." Xorek shook his head, once. "He wanted to anger me. Draw us into a trap."

"Shall we find another source? Nan-ta in Estenhorm to the south might be able to gather--"

"Too far and too slow. Even cracking the formula to free Livde has taken half a year. I will not pass another season without her by my side."

Xorek gave a smile that brought a feral light to his pale green eyes.

"No. Ursa wants us to visit, so let's oblige him. But that doesn't mean we use his front door."

STOLANSK, THE KEEP OF GRAEFE URSA, SAT ASTRIDE THE ONLY PASS through the peaks of Terranhorm Mountains, two days ride west through rolling foothills from the temple where Xorek prayed and Karvan worshipped.

Xorek and Karvan took four days to make the trip, giving themselves a wide berth about Fort Ursk, which housed the bulk of Ursa's forces on this side of the pass.

The detour meant passing among the stunted trees that grew in swaths through the foothills past the farms outlying Fort Ursk. Cooler air in the crisp fall days than they would have enjoyed on the main road, but plentiful game animals that fell easily into Karvan's snares. And the cooler air meant fewer of the makram flies to bite and pester them as they rode.

By early morning on that fifth day, Xorek and Karvan stood on the banks of the roaring Yalinsk, a rabid artery of a river, too treacherous for Ursa to exploit for trade even here, miles from the falls that carried freezing water from high in the Terranhorms. Behind them their horses, hobbled, enjoyed the sweet, thick grass.

Karvan squinted up and down the banks as far as the foothills allowed.

"Do you know some secret, safe way across this?"

"If there were a secret way, it would not be safe." Xorek clapped his friend on the shoulder. "A pointless fight against Ursa's guards and a risk of losing the element of surprise."

"Oolniph cannot carry us across that," said Karvan, his tone pointed, his face and hands chilled by spray.

"I never said he would."

Karvan sighed. Perhaps he knew how Xorek intended to cross the river.

"We'll have to leave the horses here."

"Did you plan to sneak one into Stolansk through a bolt hole?"

"Livde would not approve..."

"No? Let us ask her."

Xorek dug into a pouch at his belt and pulled out a ruby the size of his fist. Within the ruby could be seen a dark woman, beautiful in her fury, frozen mid-killing stroke with her two-handed blade.

"Livde, my love, should I use all the resources I have available to me as I try to free you from your thrice-damned prison? Or shall I restrict myself to those tools that you yourself prefer?"

"Enough," said Karvan, defeat in his voice. "I miss her too. And even she would take no issue with your imps. But demons..."

Xorek knelt close enough to the river that his knees sank into earth softened by the spray. He took his left wrist in his right hand, stared at his left palm where three ridged scars intersected.

Three scars. Three demons. Each called by a use of the Shadow-carver, the ethereal blade that carved through flesh, spirit, even the boundaries between worlds. Each then defeated, threatened, and bound for a service. Any service they could perform, so long as it did not involve battle.

A foul business, but marginally better than letting those demons run free.

Xorek stared at the scar that stretched from his middle finger to his palm, a runnel as though the flesh had been gouged by an adze. This demon's full name was Pargraavandilazaxan. Its use name was Pargrave.

The magic of the binding required Xorek to let his mind drift back to their battle. The demon's strength and fiery claws. His own shrieking sword, Shadowcarver. Finally the deep blue misty toad kneeling in submission...

It was that instant that Xorek needed. The precise moment of his mastery over this demon.

Xorek's voice and bearing reflected that dominance as his issued the call. He whispered fell Xechaglossa syllables that would reach the demon, remind it of its obligations. Demand its presence. Balance and strength suffused Xorek's pose; a slight sneer curled his lip, as though the fiend he called were a thing scraped from his boot.

A blue smear in the air. Darkening. Spreading. Finally forming the slimy shape of Pargraavandilazaxan.

"Fool," it croaked. "I will throttle you for disturbing my work and make music from your suffering."

"You will not, Pargrave," said Xorek, his voice ringing above the roar of the river. "You are bound to grant me service. I require you to transport myself and any companions I bring safely and directly across this river to the other bank, then await my return, whereupon you will transport myself and any companions I bring safely and directly back across the river to our healthy, intact, living horses."

Karvan's fingers danced along the pommel of his thin sword while the demon twisted its lips as though seeking errors in the phrasing of Xorek's demand.

Xorek showed no signs of impatience. He stood as though he could have waited for the next moon rise, left hand displaying the scars on his palm and right hand gripping his left wrist in the ritual pose.

"Very well, damnable warlock who will refuse me even tasty horseflesh. I see no companions but that skinny mouthful beside you. Or must I wait for another's arrival as well?"

"This direction only the two of us must cross."

Pargrave stretched its long, sticky tongue and wrapped it round and round the two men, then slung its tongue high and wide across the speeding froth of the river to drop them gently in the mud of the far riverbank.

The demon retracted its tongue, and each man grabbed handfuls of thick grass to rub shiny slime residue from his armor.

"Disgusting way to travel," observed Karvan.

"More comfortable than swimming," said Xorek, casting his glance up and down the hilly ridges ahead of him. Trees, but nothing more threatening than a fox.

A military man would have patrols check the river. With enough time and men, any good engineer could rig a bridge that would hold long enough for a whole arm of troops to cross.

But a money-conscious man would instead set patrols or observers farther back, at the places where the terrain would force so many men to travel.

Ursa's reputation for greed suggested that he was a money-conscious man. But the situation of his keep and his two main forts suggested their either he was a military man, or took good advice from military men.

Xorek led his companion away from the likely locations of either such arrangement of forces. The two moved up the hills along the river, the shortest route to the higher, rockier ground and the beginning of the Terranhorms proper.

THE SUN SANK LOW IN THE SKY BY THE TIME THE TWO MEN WERE working their way along the outcrops and handholds of the mountainside, some two hundred paces above the nearest hillock below them. Their straining arms and legs needed rest. Their rumbling bellies begged for something more substantial than the bits of hard tack they had allowed themselves while climbing. Perhaps the flesh of one of the mountain goats who passed so temptingly near at times. Or even one of the lattle birds, who ruined so many good handholds with their nests.

But animal flesh would have required a fire, and a fire on the mountainside would have been visible to every farm and town all the way to Fort Ursk, and beyond. Even now the two men could see fires down below. Fires at the fort. Watch fires further out.

And a fire almost directly below them, if a bit closer to the road.

When Xorek's eyes lit on that last fire, he grinned and pointed with his chin.

"Think ... we're close?" asked Karvan.

"Must be," said Xorek. "Path ... won't go straight down."

Minutes later, and a seemingly endless number of hands jammed into crevasses and boots barely hanging on to rocks entirely too small for proper support, they rounded a curve and saw two things.

The first was the sharp, imposing jut of Stolansk itself. Hewn from deep stone the mirror black of obsidian, the keep's harsh, angular towers and crenellations boasted ready ballistae and cata-pults as well as the more standard arrow slits. Any army coming up the main road would suffer heavy casualties well before moving within range of their own siege engines.

The second thing they noticed was that the mountainside cut away before them in a sharp slope, leading down to a smooth channel wide enough for a single horse and rider. On the far side of the channel, the mountain overhung, concealing this escape path from the valley below.

Xorek and Karvan slid down the slope until they landed on the swept surface of the channel.

"Anything this clean gets a lot of attention," said Karvan.

"No one sends a servant to sweep in the evening. Perhaps the guards tend to the channel on their way down to set their watch."

The overhang blocked light from the moon and stars, but as the night darkened their cautious steps up to the keep their eyes adjusted well enough for them to follow the twisting passage.

The world about them came in two shades – dark gray or black – depending on whether that space was empty or filled with rock. Karvan carried his slender sword bare in one hand. The blade bore a single edge and slight curve, but that edge was keen and the tip sharp. In his other hand he held a dagger in a throwing grip.

Xorek kept his sword hand near the bone handle of his knife, but did not touch the hilt.

The bare scrape of their boots sounded a din against the silence of the passage, as though for all their stealth they clattered like an army on the move, alerting the whole of the keep to their approach. Karvan's shoulders twitched as though expecting an arrow to split them any moment. His eyes flicked back and forth. His ears strained for any warning of an incipient ambush.

If any such concerns bothered Xorek, he did not show them. Even the hand near his bone knife never wavered.

Finally the dark gray night of the passage before them solidified into blackness. Neither man could make out any details but they had reached the bolt hole, a secret exit through which the graefe's family could escape in the event of a siege.

Ahead of them had to be a door, but whether fashioned from wood and iron or concealed among the obsidian-like rock, their eyes could not tell them.

Nor could they tell how the bolt hole might be guarded. Touching it might trigger a trap.

"Did you have a plan, Xorek?" whispered Karvan. "Or shall I knock on the wall and hope?"

"By all means, knock. Perhaps I can sneak past while the welcome party dispatches you."

But before Karvan could pitch a barbed reply, Xorek began muttering harsh syllables in the tongue of lost Xechaglossa, and rubbing his left arm three times to call forth his orange imp. Twice before that day Xorek had relied on the imp: first to find a smooth route to scale up the mountainside undetected, and second to clear a family of mountain goats from their path without making the sort of noise that echoes.

This would be Oolniph's final task before the next dawn.

The imp smeared its way to physical form before them, then immediately rubbed its hands with glee. A sickly orange glow emanated from the imp, as though its pleasure shed light.

"Lies and infidelity," it cackled. "Blood and secrets. You should call me here more often."

"Oolniph," whispered Xorek, "I charge you to open the portal before us silently, without endangering us or alerting the keep's occupants."

"Impossible," scoffed the imp. "Ask me to pluck you the moon. You'll have the same result."

"I won't tolerate your laziness, demonling. Set about your task."

"I say again, impossible. You have called up an imp to do a demon's job. Opening the door endangers you. And there is one occupant who cannot but know when the door is opened. You ask too much."

Xorek and Karvan looked toward each other, though whether either could truly see the other's expression in such scant light, none could say.

"Who or what is this occupant?" said Xorek.

"I will tell you nothing else for free. Make that my task, if you would know."

"Open the door, Oolniph, alerting only the one who cannot but know. There is your task."

"And there is your doom," said the imp.

Moments later a sliver of vertical yellow light appeared in the wall. Then it was joined by a horizontal sliver touching the top. Then the slivers grew and spread into a rectangle as a section of the wall two feet thick slid open without a hint of sound.

Inside waited a room little larger than an alcove, shaped from more shining black rock – floor, walls and ceiling – all gleaming as though wet, and lit by lamps on each wall. In the center of the room, between Xorek and Karvan and the sole door on the opposite wall, sat a Dweller.

THIS DWELLER TOOK THE FORM OF A SPIDER CARVED FROM GRAY marble; its legs long enough to enfold a horse and its pincers to crush a man's head or rib cage with equal ease. But like every other Dweller, it owed its animation to a poor human, who had his or her tortured soul flayed away through dark rituals over the course of months, each strip layered into the Dweller's power and purpose until the final breath of the victim's life became the spark of the Dweller's mockery of life, bound there further by regular treatments with noxious potions.

Xorek knew the spells to create a Dweller. He had learned many such things through the years, even if he had yet to plunge to such depths himself. Though some would call his consorting with demons just as dark.

Perhaps it was that knowledge that tightened Xorek's jaw now, sent a shiver through his shoulders.

"Password," chittered the Dweller as the two men stepped into the small room, and the word seemed to echo in the air about it.

Karvan raised his eyebrows at Xorek, but got only a head shake for his trouble.

"Password," chittered the Dweller again, and the echoes seemed to menace now as the Dweller rose to its feet, head tilted slightly.

One might almost think it wanted Xorek and Karvan to give the wrong answer. But what animated a Dweller had too little humanity left in it to want anything. A Dweller did only as it was ordered.

"I serve Graefe Ursa," ventured Xorek, one fist closed in salute over his heart.

Wrong answer.

The great spidery body pounced at them. Both men dove opposite directions, but the Dweller caught itself in the doorframe behind them and scuttled across the ceiling to block the interior door before either man could stand.

Karvan flicked a throwing dagger. It sparked off the Dweller's head. Harmless.

Xorek did not waste time on his bone-handled knife. Instead he grabbed the air above the bone hilt, twisted his hand, and drew half the form of his true blade: the Shadowcarver.

It looked like a yard of tapering metal the color of deepest twilight, with a hilt the black of a cat's pupil. No gems. No runes. No visible sign of the blade's deadly magic, only an edge in the back of the mind of every observer, like a distant scream heard somewhere between the base of the neck and the center of the skull.

"Half?" cried Karvan, barely parrying a marble leg with his slender sword and wasting another dagger thrown uselessly against the Dweller's underbelly. "We need the whole thing, Xorek!"

But Karvan did not know the burden of carrying Shadowcarver.

Xorek leapt forward, cleaving away two of the marble limbs with a single swipe of the heavy blade.

But the Dweller had six good limbs remaining. It focused on the real threat.

Six legs blurred in motion.

Xorek barely interposed the Shadowcarver between those snapping pincers and his head. Every muscle in his body strained to hold the thing back, but the Dweller had long since moved past the limitations of flesh. It possessed the relentless strength of stone now.

Back the Dweller pressed Xorek. The creature could not break the blade that restrained its pincers, and the gap in its limbs kept it from pummeling Xorek, so it tried to crush him against the far wall.

And with only half the Shadowcarver available, Xorek's armor remained mere dusky leathers.

His arms began to give. Closer and closer the marble of the pincers came until one pressed against his chest.

Pressure built. Xorek's ribs bowed. Begged for relief. But after a day on that mountain, Xorek's arms had little endurance left.

"Hah!" cried Karvan.

A stench fouled the air, like bile and old blood. The pressure eased. The pincers lost their strain. The legs began to shake.

Xorek wedged his legs behind him and shoved with all he had.

This time the Dweller gave ground. Xorek raised his enchanted sword and struck the head from its body.

The Dweller's legs kicked wildly, then the rest of the marble body collapsed.

Xorek sagged forward, braced by his sword, one hand gently probing his ribs for anything worse than a crack.

"Found the alchemy hole," said Karvan with a roguish grin. "Like you always say, 'Anything without a soul of its own has to be maintained.'"

Xorek leaned back against the wall. He thrust his sword down as though into a scabbard at his side. He twisted his hand and the blade vanished. He wiped sweat from his forehead.

"I think it bruised ... the right half of my chest. Maybe ... cracked a few."

"Did you expect less?" said Karvan closing the outer door, but not before noting the lever that had opened it. "Drawing only half the sword when we needed the whole thing. You're lucky I found the weak spot before it crushed you like a beetle."

Xorek shook his head, but said nothing.

Xorek lurched to his feet and made his way toward the interior door. Bruised and exhausted his body may have been, but he and Karvan had no time to waste. They had no way of knowing how often anyone checked on this room.

But since neither the floor nor the marble form of the former Dweller showed any signs of dust, the room had to have been attended on a regular basis.

"Where does Ursa store his jalemroot?" said Karvan, checking the door before trying the handle.

"Down by the cells, of course, where it's cool and dry."

"You know the way?"

"It's been years, but I know that bastard's cells. Intimately."

Xorek and Karvan crept down three false passages, past two sets of guards, and away from a half-dozen servants before they found the stairwell they sought: a winding, twisting cacophony of metal that would have alerted half of the keep had they assayed its stairs.

Instead they forced one more feat of climbing on their already sore and tired limbs. They made their way down the stairwell's central support pole, sliding as often as they could get away with, and working hands and feet to get themselves past impeding bends and joins.

Finally they set foot on the dull gray rock of the keep's dungeon, in a small alcove with two open doorways facing each other. Nothing like obsidian here, only slate and granite, dry and dusty and cold as Xorek and Karvan had been back on the mountainside.

They smelled old stone, stale sweat and oil, the latter coming from the lamps the builder had spaced in sconces. Lamps that flickered shadows in every corner, and kept everything else at an even dim visibility.

Of course, those lamps cast the daylight of high noon compared to the escape path Xorek and Karvan had walked to get there. The brightness of the Dweller's chamber had spoiled their night vision, but they had recovered it during their long slide and climb down the stairwell.

The lamps continued down the halls at regular intervals, but neither man could see a sign of life in either direction.

"Which way then?" asked Karvan.

"I've taken us as far as memory will help. I've been in the cells, but not the storerooms." Xorek shrugged. "The dungeons go only so far. Ursa would never risk losing his prisoners by connecting his dungeons to his mines.

"This way will do as well as the other," he said, and started down a hall.

Karvan cursed, drew his sword and a throwing dagger, and

followed. The silence and pace of his footfalls matching Xorek's out of habit.

Xorek stopped at a solid-looking wooden door on his right. His eyes narrowed as he studied the lock and frame.

"Shouldn't we have heard noise by now?" whispered Karvan.

"All this stone..." muttered Xorek. "And Ursa uses unruned wood?"

"Guards talking. Guards walking. A prisoner moaning. Something."

"*Chlatassa vin schollis.*" The ancient words seemed to sink as they left Xorek's mouth.But nothing glowed. Nothing stood revealed.

In fact, nothing seemed to happen at all.

"Xorek!" Karvan's whisper grew urgent. "Where is everyone?"

"Ursa would never leave anything as precious as jalemroot behind a few inches of wood where it could be stolen by the first imbecile with an axe. It must be further down."

"It is," said a satisfied voice from behind them.

Xorek and Karvan looked up to see the immense body of Graefe Ursa, decked out in his most ostentatious gold and purple finery. On a fitter man the clothes might have looked kingly. Instead Ursa looked more like an overdone sofa.

Surrounding the graefe stood six of his hardened soldiers, mailed, with swords and shields ready. A smaller, robed man stood next to the graefe, almost an afterthought.

"But you will never touch that jalemroot, Xorek," continued the graefe. "That you want it would be reason enough to deny you, for the trouble you've caused me in the past. That you want it to free that devil woman of yours is yet a stronger argument. But that you would break into my own keep to steal it? That is the stroke that has sealed your fate."

The insult to Livde might have fired Xorek's blood. After all, she was every bit as human as he. Perhaps more so, given the rumors about his own ancestry. But Xorek's attention was fixed on the small, robed man beside Ursa.

The beard was new. The hair shaggier. But the pinched, rat face. The haunted brown eyes. The years had not changed those.

"One betrayal was not enough, Brys? You'll take that fat fool's gold for the chance to strike at me again?"

"A man must eat," said Brys over Ursa's indignation. "And you're a fine one to speak of betrayal."

"Yes," said Ursa loud enough to draw all attention back to him. "I thought you might recognize your old friend. Do you know, I believe he is a mightier warlock than even you? Yes. In fact, I have only commissioned him to cast three spells for me. The first ... you'll see soon enough."

The graefe smiled as though his first bite of turkey leg had been cooked by the gods themselves, and he anticipated the joy of the rest of his meal.

"The second, as I'm sure you guess, allowed us to position ourselves while you traipsed right past us. And the third, well, Brys, if you would do the honors."

Brys' lips stretched back in a grimace and held up a small clay jar.

Xorek thrust his scarred left hand and rushed a chant.

Karvan threw a dagger.

Neither was fast enough. Brys smashed the jar.

A dozen imps whirled out like smoke, blurring through the air. Karvan's dagger bounced back from the cloud of imps to land in the hall before him. Thicker and thicker the air blurred until all too soon their work was done.

Xorek and Karvan were cut off from the stairwell by a wall of solid stone.

"That was our only exit," said Karvan. "Wasn't it."

"It was," said Xorek.

"You won't need it," said a voice behind them. A voice as deep as sorrow and as cold as frostbite.

Xorek and Karvan turned to see what Brys' first spell had wrought.

By the lamplight of the corridor they could first see mist, seeping in as though through cracks in the wall. Not that either man could see cracks. But the mist coalesced rapidly.

Neither man waited for the demon to form. Karvan smashed a vial near the hilt of his sword, allowing the greenish fluid within to flow down the blade and guarantee him at least one strike that could carve even the hide of a demon. More, if enough of the brew clung to the blade.

And Xorek drew the sword Shadowcarver in its entirety.

His hand seemed to clasp air above the hilt of his bone knife, but the knife vanished as he drew a yard-and-a-half blade the color of a shadow's edge. Xorek's armor rippled from dusky leathers to plates of gleaming black. Beginning with his sword hand and ending with a hood-like half-helm, he stood entirely within the sword's protection.

With one hand Xorek whipped Shadowcarver into a guard position, as though the blade weighed less than a breeze. And even that movement of the sword cut the air, a distant scream in its wake. Only enough to set the teeth on edge and tighten the shoulders of those who heard it.

But the bearer of Shadowcarver would always hear every scream echo through his body. Whether he cut armor or flesh, animal or human or demon, air, stone, or the barriers between worlds themselves, every movement of the ancient sword Shadowcarver carved something.

And what it carved died screaming.

The form the demon took was not one known to Xorek or Karvan. It seemed that Brys had studied hard since they had seen him last. The demon shaped itself like the tigers of the east, if such tigers had two sets of raking forepaws, stood eight feet at the shoulder, and sprouted three serpentine heads.

Karvan tucked away his throwing dagger, rather than waste it.

Xorek held up his weapon and his scarred left hand and said, "You see what I carry. And you see through my armor that two of your brothers are damned to my service. Withdraw to whatever hell spawned you. Withdraw or share their fate."

"You mortals always seek our favors." The demon's voice seemed to come not from its body, but from the air around them. "What boon will *you* grant *me* if I leave you alive?"

"I have not come to bargain. Withdraw or suffer."

All three snake heads snapped forward. Karvan dove into a roll that carried him past the demon. Xorek jumped to the side, evading one head. He whipped his sword across, shrieks in its wake as it cut another head's jaw in half.

The lost bit of demon reverted to mist and funneled into the blade.

But dodging the heads had left Xorek vulnerable to a blindingly fast forepaw. Raking claws screeched across armor plates, scarring but not piercing. Still, the force of the blow knocked Xorek from his feet.

Fire burned through Xorek's chest. His ribs had suffered a great deal of punishment against the Dweller, and that last blow felt as though it cracked what had been bruised. Each breath felt constricted. But after that initial flare, the pain felt distant.

Karvan made to slice at a tiger haunch, but its tail knocked him aside with more strength than so thin an appendage should have. Karvan was forced to catch himself against the wall, ignored as the demon moved in after the fallen Xorek.

Two heads snapping. One head thrusting like a battering ram. Two claws swiping. And all of them coming at the fallen Xorek.

Xorek tucked his knees and rolled backward to his feet, narrowly avoiding the strikes, and swinging with both hands he carved two heads from the demon, their death cries echoing through his skull and bones. He would hear those cries again and again through the years, for the worst of the screams haunted his dreams.

Such was the burden of Shadowcarver's bearer.

But even as the fallen heads turned to mist and flowed into the fell blade, the demon recovered its feet. Its lone, jawless head weaved in circles, tail slashing and free claws kneading the air as they waited for flesh to rend.

"Kneel," demanded Xorek with as much command as he could muster with so little breath. To make his point he menaced the fiend with his sword, its screams still echoing in the close hallway. "You ... are beaten..."

The demon looked from Xorek to Karvan and back. Perhaps it weighed its chances, even though it now lack the worst of its weapons. And with some of its flesh lost to Shadowcarver, retreat was no longer possible. If defeated, its choices had been reduced to bondage or permanent death.

The demon knelt.

"I'll have ... your name..." said Xorek.

Karvan shoved his sword hilt deep into the demon's belly and carved his way out. The demon fell dead as the stone floor beneath it.

"You have too many demons already," said Karvan. "You can get by without one more."

Xorek stared at the demon corpse. Perhaps he considered harvesting the specific parts that were called for by certain dark rituals. Or perhaps those were rituals that even Xorek would hesitate to work.

"You just denied us a resource we may need someday."

"Perhaps," admitted Karvan. "But not a resource we need today."

Behind the unlocked doors in the corridor, Xorek and Karvan found sacks of wheat and barley, dried meats and salted fish, barrels of water and wine, bolts of rough and fine fabrics, and other supplies that one might expect to find in emergency stores. Not nearly enough to supply the whole of the keep, these must have been additional supplies for the graefe's family themselves, and perhaps the most special and important of their retainers.

They left those doors open behind them, adding such air as they could to what they had available, however stale it might taste.

They found only one locked door between the newly added stone wall and the old stone of the corridor's end, and that door had a triple-lock, disguised to look as though it held no locks at all.

Even Karvan, a surer hand with the picks than Xorek, must have taken half an hour to find and open those locks.

Not that anyone could have told time, except by the flickering of the lamps. They looked to have held enough oil to burn for six hours, if full, but neither Xorek nor Karvan had any way of knowing how long they had been burning.

Still, when the last of those locks clicked open, Karvan smiled, stepped back, and gestured to the door with a flourish.

Xorek pulled free his bone-handled knife, grasped the door handle, twisted, and shoved.

The door remained closed.

"You missed a lock," said Xorek.

"I didn't," insisted Karvan. "I've been over the whole thing twice, door and frame and stone around it." He pointed. "That door is unlocked."

"Magic then," said Xorek with a sigh. "A permission seal, and we don't have permission."

Xorek thrust his knife back into its sheath with an irritated shove.

"Perhaps you could..." began Karvan, but too late.

Xorek drew the full Shadowcarver and cut the door free from its frame, slashing right through the locks, the wood, the stone, the magic, the very essence of the space the door occupied. The keening in the blade's wake grated along the nerves of both men, but sharpest down the spine of Xorek himself.

The door fell to the floor, but before the rent in space could heal itself, out popped a demon.

This one was small, eight-limbed, and covered in fur the green shade of bad meat. Little more than an imp, it was quickly dispatched with a single thrust of Karvan's blade.

Xorek opened his mouth to say something, but Karvan cocked an eyebrow, almost daring him to complain. Instead Xorek shook his head. He grabbed a flickering lamp from the wall and led the way into the now-open storeroom.

The storeroom was cavernous, like the others, shaped and flattened floor and walls up to the natural curves and hanging rocks just within the dim edge of sight. Likely all of the rooms on this side of the corridor had once been part of a single cave, partitioned off for the graefe's convenience.

But though the other rooms had been stacked high and tight with goods, this room contained no barrels, no sacks, no crates. It contained only a priceless pile of jalemroot, perhaps three pounds worth, in the center of the room. More than had ever been assembled before anywhere on the continent.

The jalemroot glittered like the gold that spawned it, tough and gnarled in lengths that, even stretched, would look shrunken beside a man's smallfinger.

Xorek measured and separated a half-pound's worth, enough to ransom a Southern king or perhaps three well-loved high lords.

"Gather the rest," said Xorek. "Prepare it for travel while I work."

"Shouldn't we get someplace safe first?"

"I won't leave her trapped a moment longer than I must."

"How are we going to get out of here, anyway?"

Xorek did not look up from arranging the piles of jalemroot into seven points around the ruby. Instead he displayed his scarred left hand to remind his friend that two demons still owed him favors.

Outside the seven points of jalemroot, Xorek arranged and lit a triangle of candles: red, silver and brown, the three colors of the soul. He then drew his bone-handled knife and slashed open his unscarred right palm, dribbling the flow of blood in a circle around the triangle.

Jalemroot for transformation. Fire to call back the soul. Blood of the belovéd to restore the body. Three kinds of incense, each dragged through the blood of his palm before being drizzled over the appropriate candle: savory over the red, sweet over the brown, and sharp over the silver.

Finally came the words. Words that Xorek and Karvan had hunted down for months in many a lonely tomb and forbidden tower, crossing barren waste and sour sea alike for fragments of the incantation. Fragments that Xorek had to assemble himself, for this goal was too precious to trust to the chance of a demon's lie.

Xorek spread his arms and began to chant. Deep and ululating, the words seemed to draw from the depths of Xorek's very being, pulling at whatever passed for his soul, stretching it from his toes up along his spine, down from his head and out through his hands, weaving a portion of himself around the blood circle before him.

Karvan found that his hands stopped their gathering as the rolling sounds of the chant made their way down through his body. His eyes swept toward the ruby in its triple-structure, turning his head and shoulders sharply to bring it into view.

The air about them shook as Xorek chanted the seven repetitions of the spell, the syllables running along the floor and through the very walls.

Blood on Xorek's hands from the cut. Blood in Xorek's sweat from the spell. He began to grow lightheaded, the room seeming to brighten about him, though Karvan saw no such difference. Xorek's arms and back strained as though he lifted the whole of the keep and the caverns from his place there within the mountain.

At last the final word of the seventh repetition rolled out of him with a snap that shuddered through Xorek to his core. He dropped forward onto his knees, pain roiling through his chest, the taste of blood on his tongue.

The ruby vanished, as did the jalemroot, the candles, even the circle of blood. And where they stood appeared Livde, the Scourge of Draymark Pass, the Devil of the Deep Wastes, poised for combat in her leathers and her naked sword in both hands, mid-swing.

"--nable cur! I'll ... Xorek!"

Livde dropped her sword and took her slumped, bloody lover in her arms. "Who has done this to you? Where--"

"His sorcery did that to him, Livde," said Karvan, stretching the muscles that had kinked while he had knelt, locked in position. "You were caught in a ruby trap."

Karvan managed an echo of his roguish smile despite the discomfort all through his body.

"Hello, by the way."

"Well met, old friend," Livde said, still cradling the barely conscious Xorek. "But a ruby trap? That's just a legend."

"A legend that Kolvin Thrice-Dead pieced together. Took us the better part of a year to chase down the trick of freeing you."

"Is that ... jalemroot beside you?"

"All that Ursa had," said Karvan with a wave of his hand, "minus what Xorek needed for the spell."

Livde began cleaning the blood from Xorek's face and hands with a bit of old horse rag from her belt, and the process seemed to revive him.

"Livde?" Xorek said, his first word weak but his voice growing stronger as he continued, "then it worked?"

"It worked, my love. And thank you." She kissed him, and as the kiss stretched on Karvan chuckled to himself, as though all were right with the world again.

When the kiss finally ended, Livde looked fondly into Xorek's eyes and said, "Even if it took you a good season longer to free me from this than I needed to save you from the dungeons beneath Khol Keep."

"This involved ancient magic," insisted Xorek, coming to his feet.

"That keep had a dragon. Did you have to face a dragon?"

Karvan could not contain his laughter now as the debate of deeds went back and forth, a competition that always seemed to inflame their desire. He did not interrupt them until he had safely packed away every scrap of the remaining jalemroot. By the time he looked up, Xorek and Livde looked ready to cast aside their armor and culminate their reunion.

"I hate to intrude on a moment that grows more and more private," said Karvan, "but there's still the small matter of getting us past that wall Brys' imps made."

"Brys is working for Ursa?" said Livde, not quite breathless.

"So it seems," said Xorek, irritation setting his jaw. He raised his left hand and pointed at a scar. "But this demon can take us anywhere I have traveled since the last full moon, so long as I do not ask it to cross water. It will be able to get us past that wall and out of the keep in safety."

"More demons, Xorek? I leave you alone for a few months--"

"Well if you like that," said Karvan, "you'll love the one he called to carry us back across the river to our horses. How do you feel about toad spit?"

Livde's expression darkened, but Xorek smiled.

"I could always cut through Brys' wall with Shadowcarver. Would you rather face the archers Ursa must have waiting for us? Shouldn't be more than a forearm's worth. Personally, I favor Ursa taking down the wall himself and finding us long gone, and with us his precious jalemroot."

"Good market for it in Estenhorm," added Karvan.

"Well," said Livde with a slow smile, "I *would* rather celebrate my freedom..."

Xorek called his demon to spirit them away.

SPELL BURNT AND
SLEEPLESS

Old words. Venya was still in training when she heard them the first time. Learned the truth of them herself when she was still a squire. When she still hoped to be a knight. She'd carried news from the front to some second or third son of a duke, and he'd blamed *her* for a battle turning against him.

Old words that came back to her now, as warriors melted out of the forest of evergreens on either side of the wide dirt road. Too much like wolves on the hunt for Venya's liking.

And timed well.

The afternoon sun was less than an hour from setting over the Ironspike Mountains in the distance. Be in her eyes in a fight. The spring air already cooling, as though evening were closer than the rich blue of the sky made it look.

Venya's attention had flagged. Thoughts of dinner in her pack, the leftover roast lamb, with its lemon and basil.

The warriors wore chainmail, down to the coifs. Recently oiled, from the smell overlaying the scent of the evergreens. No badges or standards on their shields or shoulders. Longswords that looked dinged and nicked here and there, but keen enough and held steady. Round shields from a thick hardwood.

No archers, though.

Unless they had an archer tucked away among those trees.

If so, they'd prove it soon enough.

The six she could see had a hard, weathered look to them. Not one could have seen fewer than thirty summers, but none of them looked to have seen the forty she'd seen.

Venya had a longsword too, and hers was in better shape. And a steel, kite shield, strapped to the saddle of Starfall, her great black destrier. No chainmail, but good leather with steel studs, and a small dagger tucked into the long braid of her black hair.

And she had a few tricks no one ever taught warriors. She just hoped she didn't need them.

She knew she looked as weathered as they did. Knew they wouldn't see any more mercy in her blue eyes than she saw in the brown eyes of the one she pegged as their leader. His armor looked a little cleaner. He stood a step closer.

And he just had that air of command, the way some did.

"If you're looking for an easy mark," she said, "there's a caravan about an hour behind me. Probably already stopped for the night. Spices, but the merchant's too cheap to hire good help. You could—"

"We're not after spices," said the leader, his voice as rough and weathered as his skin. Had a scar down one cheek too. Reminded Venya of the first man who assumed she couldn't wield the sword she carried. "And we're not after your virtue either."

"My son will be glad to hear it. Every boy still believes his mother a maiden."

"You know what we're after. Don't make us kill you for it."

Venya did know. A sheaf of papers the spice merchant considered too important to wait for his caravan. Important enough to pay Venya as much as he paid the rest of his caravan guards combined, "just to get it to Devanor early."

"I'd hand it over," she said, "but I'm afraid I just love the taste of lamb too much to give my dinner to the likes of you."

The leader raised his sword.

An arrow slammed into the dirt near Starfall's hooves.

So much for words.

A quick pat to the right spot on the neck and Starfall leapt to a gallop, riding down the man unfortunate enough to stand in the center of the road.

An arrow zoomed past behind her.

Venya cut down at the leader as she passed. Her sword only took a chunk from his shield.

The hired sword to her left couldn't get into position in time for a strike before she was past him.

The arrows came from the north. Venya led Starfell south, off the road and close to the tree line.

An arrow punched her ribs, but deflected off a steel stud in her leather. Leave a hell of a bruise come morning, but better that than her lung.

Venya reined Starfall to a halt just inside the tree line. Out of sight for no more than a moment, but a moment was all she needed.

Venya dismounted, grabbed her shield, dropped her sword and lay a hand on the side of the destrier's head. Then she wrenched her mouth and throat through two syllables of ancient Iktish, a tongue never meant for human tongues.

The word burned its way out of her, rasping along her throat and leaving a trail of purple smoke from her singed lips.

But the spell did its job. Starfall and the sheaf of papers merged with the trees. No mere fairy glamor or elf trick, this. Horse, pack, papers, all were part of the trees now, and would be until Venya unmade the spell. Or someone more powerful than her.

Now she had five more hired swords to deal with. And an archer. If the fool wasn't smart enough to run.

———

Venya crouched among the thick underbrush. Sword in one hand, shield in the other. The bushes surrounding her were prickly and smelled sweet. Sweeter than their little red berries, which weren't any more poisonous than they were tasty. They were tart, and something in their undertaste reminded Venya of blood.

But chewing them forced Venya to slow down. To let the warriors make the mistakes that would prove their undoing.

The warriors fanned out. They would know she could not have gotten far. No horse could ride easily through these thick woods. The evergreens grew too wide and too close together, and below them the underbrush held too many vines that could break a horse's leg.

"We just want the papers," called the leader again. The only one not entering the woods, looking for her. Even his archer had left his hiding place and come to join his commander.

The archer was younger. Maybe her son Vintas' age, which made him about half Venya's age.

He didn't have the same hard look as his fellows. Maybe he could be reasoned with.

"Here!"

Seventh Hell, Venya'd wasted too much time comparing the archer to her son. Missed one of the hired swords getting damn near close enough to stab her. No more than a long stride away from her. This one had the same brown eyes as the leader. Might have been a younger brother. But he had three warts on his chin.

Venya came up shield high as Three Warts swung down at her.

But Venya didn't do the expected. She didn't stand to meet her foe on even footing (even though her footing would have been far from uneven, there among the brambles of the red berry plant).

Instead she held her shield above her and dove forward. Her sword stabbing for his guts. Her tip bloodied him, but his chainmail held. Kept the stab from opening more than a thumb-length of his belly.

His sword bounced off her shield. Venya landed hard on the needles and dirt just inside the forest's edge. Rolled. His blade was coming again. Awkward. A little slow.

Venya swung hard at his arm. His chainmail saved his arm, but she heard and felt his wrist break.

Footsteps incoming, the last she could hear before his screaming started.

Venya rolled to her feet.

Two close enough to fight now. A third coming in.

Venya slipped back and forth between the two closest. Parrying blows with sword and shield, but trying nothing more than a feint herself. Here within the trees she needed nothing more than their proximity to make an end of this.

The third joined the fight.

Venya put her back to a tree that stood between her and the road. No chance of an arrow catching her here. And, if the ones on the road were lucky, they wouldn't see what happened next.

Venya sucked the taste of the berries to the roof of her mouth. Tart, almost bloody.

The three gave each other enough space that all three could attack. A tight half circle in front of her.

Just what she wanted.

Venya forced herself to cough up two more words of Iktish. Bad idea, casting two spells in such quick succession, but a better idea than dying.

The words boiled first in her guts and lungs, drenching her in foul-smelling sweat as they scalded up her throat to her poor, singed lips.

The words came out as violet smoke that seeped into the steel held by the three hired swords in front of Venya. Into every link of their chainmail, into the blades and hilts of their swords. Into any daggers they carried.

All of it.

And every bit of that metal bubbled like acid and burned away the flesh beneath it. The three men died screaming as their own weapons and armor ate them down to the bone.

Venya forced herself to watch their flesh boil away. To hear their screams. To see what he magic wrought, that she never forget that the toll it exacted was not only on her own person.

And that toll was bad enough. She could feel the shakiness of her sword hand. The fire burning down to embers in her lungs. She could smell the oily foulness of her own sweat mingling with the odors of roast flesh and molten metal.

Her lips still smoked purple, and felt sore and cracked.

Only her tongue, the instrument that shaped those unnatural words, remained unblemished by her sorcery. As though the spells refused to harm the part she needed to form them.

Venya turned and stepped from the woods. Sword and shield held high. Her head lighter than it should have been, given the weight of what she'd just seen.

But not for the lives of the hired swords. They were little more than bandits, and deserved what they got.

The remainder of their band was waiting in the road. The leader, sword and shield at the ready. The archer, hand near his quiver and bow ready. And Three Warts, crying and holding his wrist. His sword and shield were gone. Probably still in the woods.

"Your men are dead," she said, voice dry and rough like desert sand. "Leave or join them."

"Kill her," said the leader to his archer.

Venya gave the archer The Look.

The Look was something every warrior developed, sooner or later. It was a way of saying, without words, "Don't make me kill you. We both know I can and will."

The archer dropped his bow.

"Coward!" yelled the leader, raising his sword. The archer squeezed his eyes tight shut, unwilling to watch his own death come for him.

"Kill him and you die next," said Venya, stepping closer.

The leader stopped and looked at her.

The archer opened his right eye, as though if he opened both he'd find out he was dreaming and the leader's sword was about to cut the head from his body.

But Venya couldn't take her eyes off the leader. She'd already let herself get caught once unawares today. She might not survive a second mistake.

"Archer," she said. "Do you have horses?"

"Yes," he said.

"Get them," she said. "We'll need them."

The archer ran back for the tree line, his bow all but forgotten on the ground at his leader's feet.

"You *have* a horse," said the leader. "A better one than ours."

"Had," Venya said. "Tried a spell to let us pass through the underbrush like it was air. Worked for the horse. Not for me."

The leader's jaw dropped open. A harsh laugh barked out of him.

Venya glared. "Stop that laughing or I'll gut you for spite. You idiots just cost me my mount and my courier's fee. I'll never see that damned horse again, much less those papers. So I'm taking your horses for my trouble."

"And my archer?"

"I think you're going to kill him the moment I'm not around to stop you. So he comes with me."

"And you're letting us two go?"

"Soon as you drop your sword, and the two daggers I can see." Venya smiled. "And the one in your boot that I *can't* see."

The leader raised his sword and shield.

"Three Warts there isn't going to be any help to you now. And you heard the death screams of the others. You can go look at their melted bodies, if you like. That kind of sorcery I'm *very* good at."

The leader threw down his sword in disgust. Then his shield. His daggers followed.

"Keep the shield," she said. "All kinds of bandits on this road, it seems."

The leader clenched his teeth hard as he picked up his shield. Probably swallowing some painful words. But the leader and Three Warts started walking back down the road about the time the archer came back with the horses.

The leader wasn't kidding. They were all right, for rounceys, but nothing on Starfall.

"This way," she said, taking charge of the horses and leading them off the road. The sun was going down soon, and they needed to make camp. "Grab the weapons."

"How do you know I won't kill you?" said the archer.

Venya looked at him. So like her own Vintas. The green-gold eyes, the set to his lips.

"Because you'd rather ride with me than them. Because you know I'm a better warrior, you know I'm a sorceress, and because you know I'm not going to kill you for doing the smart thing."

The archer nodded. "I'm Kalta."

"Venya."

She led him next to the evergreens on the south side of the road and helped him hobble the horses.

"Should I get a fire going?" he said.

"No," she said. "The moon will be bright tonight, and I want leagues between us and any reinforcements your old leader can call up."

"There won't be any," said Kalta. "He's two days from the man who hired us. He could never get there and reach us again before we get to Devanor. And anyway, you don't have the papers, so—"

"That's not exactly true," Venya said.

She led Kalta to the right trees, and broke the spell with a single, painful word.

That was too much for one day. Venya's belly burned, and so did her lungs and mouth. And her lips would not stop smoking.

"Get the fire going," she said through a grimace. "We're staying here tonight after all.

Kalta turned to obey.

Venya followed, slowly, leading Starfall who seemed the only one to make it through today's misadventure none the worse for wear.

Venya could scarce taste her lamb that night, which was perhaps the saddest thought of all. Kalta seemed to enjoy it, at least, and he slept the untroubled sleep of one who has never killed. He could not have been traveling with his old group very long.

Killing no longer kept Venya from sleeping, but she could not close her eyes that night. Knew she would perhaps not sleep tomorrow night either. Too much magic, done too soon. The fires would burn inside her until the spells eased their way out.

***

THE REST OF VENYA'S RIDE TO DEVANOR WAS SMOOTH. SHE REACHED the town before sundown that next day, on the banks of the Eldriss River. Hard packed dirt for the city streets. Devanor had some lord with a keep on the closest thing the town had to a hill. The rest of the town was an assortment of one and two story buildings, made from wood or stone depending on how much money the people inside had.

The woman Venya delivered the papers to had a stone house, with windows of leaded glass, and four guards outside that Venya could see without trying.

And then her task was finished.

An easy enough job. Except that she'd had to kill four men.

Except that she could still feel the Iktish sorcery burning at her guts. Turning the taste of her food to ash. Flavoring the sweet spring air with cinders. Keeping her sleepy eyes open and roiling through her insides.

And it seemed as though she'd adopted a new son.

She'd expected Kalta to go his own way once they reached Devanor, but he looked at Venya like she was his new leader.

Not so much like Vintas then. Vintas was no follower. Still…

She turned to face Kalta outside Yolen Stables in the market square, where she'd gotten a fair price for five of the rounceys. Night was coming on soon, and they'd need an inn. And *two* rooms, just to make sure matters stayed clear between them, in his head.

"All right," Venya said. "You can ride with me as long as you prove yourself useful."

"I'm good with my bow," he said quickly, but then, slower, said, "But I've never killed anything but game animals."

"Nothing wrong with hunting. Better profession than killing."

"But I want—"

"If you say to be a knight, you're following the wrong woman. I'm not knight."

"No. You're a sorceress. Maybe you could teach me that?"

Venya almost said no. She almost *laughed*, and said no. But then it occurred to her that if Kalta knew a little sorcery, he could have freed Starfall from the trees and she might be able to sleep tonight, and taste food.

"All right," she said with a slow nod. "First lesson. Courier work is for suckers."

THE BROKEN WAND

Down at the end of Killers' Row, past the point where the cobblestones gave way to raw dirt, there was one last tavern huddled under the great granite walls of the monastery.

To be honest, I think the monastery forgot it was even there. Not that monks of the Great Raven had any proscriptions against drinking. They were some of the best customers of the lower end taverns in the area. They drank copiously, told jokes that even made the sailors blush, and though those monks didn't start trouble, with a single coughing cry they could end it.

Of course, it helped that a single coughing cry from one Raven Brother was enough to summon twenty or thirty more Raven Brothers. A veritable murder of monks.

Hence the street name, Killers' Row.

But the Raven Brothers ignored that last little tavern for the same reason most other drinkers ignored it. The worn, wooden sign depicting a stick, snapped in two by a pair of pale hands.

The tavern was called the Broken Wand. And it existed for guys like me.

I got there just after dusk that night, and already the place was packed. Of course, for the Broken Wand, that meant it was half-full.

Gray stone for the whole place. Irregular chunks mortared together, as though Morty, the owner, built the place from the leftovers of what went into building the monastery. Kept it cool in the summer, but on a rainy autumn night like this, it was damp and chilly. A fire flickered in the hearth along the left-hand wall, but the poor little flame wasn't much more than decoration.

On nights like this, the Broken Wand reminded me of my rooms in my old master's tower. Would've thought a great wizard like Melifala – yes, that Melifala, and yes, she had all the cold beauty the bards sing of, and no, she's not taking on any new apprentices – would have given her apprentice more welcoming chambers. Maybe I was supposed to have made them warmer and more welcoming through my mastery of her teachings.

Or maybe she just never liked me. Tough call.

Anyway, I shivered as much with recognition as with chill as I closed the heavy wooden door behind me. Little smell of beer. Stronger smell of roast pork.

At shadowy, candle-lit tables scattered around the tavern, fifteen sets of eyes flicked up to check out the newcomer.

Recognition in about half those eyes. Welcome in none of them.

Price of my job.

Owners of those eyes ranged from youths just getting their beards to older types who probably felt the damp chill reflected their own deep sadness. Men and women both, and some who might have been either or both. Didn't matter. I wasn't there for what might or might not have been between anyone's legs. Not that night, anyway.

Morty looked up at me from behind the bar and his face went as sour as his beer. Morty was a bald guy, with the kind of sag to his frame that came with running a tavern and always sampling this or that or some other thing.

I smiled at that sour look. I had the kind of smile that gleamed out of my neatly trimmed black beard. I liked to think it made me look devilishly handsome. More likely it made me look like an arrogant son of a bitch.

Anyway, Morty obviously didn't want me here, but he didn't want to yell across the room and annoy his customers. Hard to keep of the pretense of mystery if the barman hollered like it was any other bar. Morty'd wait and watch for now, so I swept my eyes over the crowd again.

A few of the patrons shifted uncomfortably. Always a good sign. Guilty consciences spilled their secrets fast as a Raven Brother could spill beer.

I saw three pairs of red eyes. None of them natural, of course. That bit about born wizards being marked by glowing red eyes is just a sailor's tale.

Unfortunately, none of those red eyes belonged to the man I was looking for.

Any other tavern, I would have cleared my throat and addressed the whole room. Maybe held up a handful of fire to impress the ignorant. But even failed wizards knew better than to be impressed by that trick. And anyway, talking to the whole room at once would have blown the atmosphere for Morty.

So I held up empty hands instead, kept up that smile, like I was just here for a drink.

I could feel some of them watching me as I made my way across the uneven floor. No magic to that. Just the kind of awareness I developed after the first time someone tried to kill me. A little more threat coming from my left. Looking would have been a mistake though, so I kept my eyes on the bar.

No one sat at the bar, of course. No mystery in sitting at a bar. I was probably the first patron in at least a month to plant his butt on a wooden stool.

Morty shoved a clay mug of beer at me, then turned and went into the back while his waiters came out to make the rounds among the tables. His waiters were a pair of identical twins who acted like his kids, but must have had a beautiful mother. They had that androgynous look: fine bones, fine skin, fine, light brown hair down to their shoulders. Slender frames, even though they both had to be of age.

Clay mug, not pewter. Beer, not waiting for an order. No smile. No greeting. Didn't even wait for a coin before heading into the back. Yeah, Morty was telling me to drink up and get gone.

That wasn't all, though, of course. He was telling me he wasn't going to give me any help.

Poor sap probably didn't realize he was also telling me he knew something about my quarry.

Well, I'd get back to Morty. Had a whole room full of people to talk to first.

I turned back to face the room. Toasted the sets of calculating eyes still looking at me, and sipped the sour beer.

Ruined the moment by making a face, but there was nothing I could do about that. Never expected Morty to give me his bottom-of-the-barrel stuff.

He must have really wanted me gone.

"You're not welcome here, Karzax," said one of the red-eyed men, sitting off to my right as I faced the room. "You gave up that right when you started hunting us."

Two tables away, by the wall. Maybe fifteen paces.

"Not you, Yarlson," I said, still sitting. "Not tonight, anyway. Not unless you've done something more recent than that fake potion you sold to—"

"*That potion was real!*" Yarlson thumped the table with his fist.

Me, I'm a bigger guy than most wannabe-wizards. Big enough and strong enough that when my wand got broken, Melifala wanted me to stay on and train as a man-at-arms.

Yarlson, though, he was bigger than me. And he definitely looked angrier.

"My mistake," I said, smiling again in a way that left no doubt about my own opinion in the matter. "Doesn't matter, though. Not to me, anyway. That was the accusation, and that was the reason I brought you in. You had your day in court, right?"

Yarlson nodded so sharply, it was like he tried to punch me across the room, using his heavy jaw. No way to tell from that if he'd been found guilty or innocent. But for this conversation, I knew what I'd pretend to assume.

"So. No harm done. Now the guy I'm here about tonight..."

"I haven't sold a potion since." Yarlson's red eyes took on a dark tinge, and his voice got echo-y in a way that would definitely have impressed a farmer. "And that's—"

"Not my fault," I said, steel in my voice now. "I didn't make the charge. I didn't do anything but bring you in. Now, the guy I'm here about..."

I let the words trail off because three other people stood up. One man, one woman, and one I wasn't sure about. All had red eyes, like they'd all suffered the same mishap in training.

And all four of them advanced.

WOODEN CHAIRS SCRAPED ON THE UNEVEN GRANITE FLOOR. THOSE JUST here to drink abandoned their tables – and any risk of being found mysterious – and headed for the outer ring of tables, closest to the walls. The waiters slipped back behind the bar like they'd never left it. One of them reached for my mug, but I held it out of reach.

Yarlson and his cronies approached. Stopped about two paces away.

Already had my plan in mind. Throw the beer in Yarlson's face. Smash the clay mug against the face of the androgynous person to his right. With my other hand throw my stool into the gut of the next man in line. Then turn to face the woman. If I was still standing.

"Turning on your own," Yarlson said, voice dripping with scorn. "What's the first thing we were all taught as apprentices?"

All three of his cronies answered in unison.

"Wizards are their own law."

"Yeah," I said, "well, none of us are wizards, are we? I mean, we come *here* because every one of us failed. Which is why you were hocking 'potions' to farmers, and why I'm working for the mayor's office."

"We'll see," Yarlson said. "We'll see who's a wizard and who isn't."

"Sure," I said. "Well, you're not holding a rod or a staff, so show me your wand. And I don't mean—"

Yarlson held up a handful of pale blue fire. The ghost of a real flame.

"Match me," he said.

"Doesn't prove anything," I said, and for the life of me I couldn't keep the tension out of my voice. "We all failed along the way. So—"

"Match me or admit you don't belong here and leave."

All three of his cronies nodded, but that was to be expected. I glanced past them at the rest of the room. I could see the answer in the eyes looking back at me. Pride. Wounded pride, but pride nonetheless. They'd all failed – either the final test like me, or sometime before then – or they wouldn't be drinking in this tavern.

But they didn't want to admit the failure. They wanted to cling to the image of themselves as wizards.

And none of them were going to talk to me unless I matched Yarlson.

"Fine," I said with a sigh. I put down my beer. Then I raised my voice. "Two conditions. One, everyone here stands witness, not just these three. And if I win—"

"No conditions," Yarlson said. "Match me or leave."

I got at least half of what I wanted though. The others in the room started forward. At least I would have enough witnesses that *some* of them were bound to be fair.

I stood. I raised a handful of that same ghostly fire.

I clapped my fiery hand with Yarlson's.

The room vanished.

YARLSON AND I STOOD INSIDE A WORLD OF GHOSTLY BLUE FIRE. UNDER our boots it seemed to be solid enough, and formed a circle about ten paces wide. The edges, though, were flame that wouldn't burn our flesh, but our essence.

Just past the veil of fire, I could make out the eyes of our witnesses, watching with wizard sight from the physical world, where our two bodies stood, joined at the hand. And all of the patrons could see us. Wizard sight was the first skill taught to any apprentice. Half the patrons at the Broken Wand probably couldn't have called the blue fire, much less entered the matching circle, but they could all watch.

In this place, Yarlson and I looked like misty versions of ourselves. Colorless, save for a vaguely white translucence.

This place, the matching circle, was where true wizards resolved their differences. Where they could fling whatever spells they wished, without risking their priceless possessions or, worse, an innocent countryside. For Yarlson and me to come here felt like the height of arrogance. But maybe that was the point.

The smell of the place was ambergris. I never understood why.

Yarlson smiled at me. His features began to melt and change. A smaller frame. Long, pale hair. Wide features and no beard.

Not the potion-hawker after all. This was Hristoffur.

My quarry.

This was bad. If I'd been in my own body right then, I probably would have felt my stomach seize. Hell, the ghost of my stomach tried to seize. Hristoffur had been a wizard. Full-fledged, wand-wielding magic user. For all of about six months before he'd started kidnapping peasants for experimentation.

His own master – Gord the Maker – brought him down. Snapped his wand. "Dealt" with him. And that might have been the end of it. Except that apparently there were ways for a broken wizard to recover his power. From what I'd been told, the avenue Hristoffur was pursuing required him to could catch the life force of thirteen people and thrust it into a wand or staff or rod. Some properly prepared vehicle.

He'd killed two by the time the mayor found out. Sent me in, because without his wand he was still a failed wizard. Couldn't do anything more than I could, so nothing I couldn't handle. Not in the living world of flesh and blood, anyway.

But here, in the matching ground, in one of the Places Between. Here he had power like I had good looks.

And me, I only had what I had.

In terms of magic, that meant I had squat compared to him. But I did have one edge he didn't know about.

"So," I said, "does this mean you won't come quietly? Because—"

I had to duck under a ball of fire. There were ways to call up magical shields. I even knew one or two. But I didn't think Hristoffur would give me the minute or so I'd need to do it.

I dodged left. Slid under the snap of a lightning whip.

Never thought of my own fireballs as small or pathetic. Not until I saw one of my own after ducking the third of Hristoffur's. His were a good foot across. Burned so hot that even here the air sizzled as they passed. Mine weren't half that size, and felt tepid in comparison.

But I threw three in quick order. Hristoffur caught the first with his lightning whip, but had to conjure a water disc to block the next two.

Bought me a second to dig in the echo of my pouch for the tool I needed.

Turned out I didn't have a whole second. I'd looked away at the wrong moment.

Pain scalded every nerve of my body. Even my teeth hurt. Even my hair hurt. He'd caught me by the ankles with that lightning whip. Yanked my feet out from under me.

The fall didn't hurt. Not compared to the waves of pain shooting through my system from the whip. I could smell my own essence burning.

Ambergris. Huh.

Something about that scent, that moment of realization, snapped me past the pain in a way that my old master never got me to do. I had a flash of clarity like I'd never experienced before.

The pain. The pain was still there, but it was as distant as my own body, just then. I could hear Hristoffur's laugh of triumph. Hear the certainty of his victory. Hear that in his own head he'd beaten me as was already moving on to what he'd do next. I could see that he'd dropped his water shield. Dropped any worry about defense. In his free hand he held a curved ebon dagger, glowing with red runes.

The bastard planned to make me one of his thirteen. Right here in front of over a dozen witnesses.

But the scent of ambergris. I understood then that it was the smell of magic. That this place, this matching circle, was pure magic. That here, even our bodies were composed of pure magic.

That was the secret of the matching circle. Why all spells were freely available. Everything here was already magic. Only will could be harmed here. Only the selves we brought with us.

The lightning whip around my ankles. It was as much a part of Hristoffur as his own hands. In this place.

I pulled from my bag the cold iron cuff. The witch iron. The magic dampener. The tool of the true wizard hunter, on lone to me only because my quarry was so close to being a true wizard.

Hristoffur's expression shifted from joyous celebration to confusion.

I clapped the iron around his lightning whip.

The matching circle melted away.

ONCE MORE I STOOD IN THE COLD DAMP OF THE BROKEN WAND. Fourteen failed wizards watching from one side, two androgynous waiters watching from behind the bar.

My right hand clasped to Hristoffur's right hand. His features here must have returned to their natural form when they did in the matching circle.

My witch iron clasped around his left wrist.

"No!" Hristoffur cried.

"Yes," I said, and slammed my forehead into his nose. Felt the satisfying crunch and the trickle of hot wetness that followed.

Hristoffur fell. Dazed, but one hand reaching for a weapon. Probably the dagger.

I didn't give him time to get it. I held tight to the witch iron with one hand, and beat him senseless with the other. I just kept punching and punching until my knuckles hurt like hell and I was sure he was unconscious.

Only then did I look up at his three cronies. They had their hands raised, backing away under my glare.

"Thought he was Yarlson," said the man, and the other two nodded. "Not workin' with *him*. Swear it."

I nodded. Didn't really care though. I mostly wanted to make sure no one intended to stick a knife in me while I rifled through Hristoffur's possessions for that wicked dagger. Not to mention anything else that felt like it had even a trace of magic.

I'd turn it all over. I just didn't want him using any of it on me.

I hoisted up Hristoffur's unconscious body over my shoulder like a sack of grain, back on the farm where I grew up.

"Next time," I said, trying not to pant for breath, "remember I'm the guy *stopping* guys like him. Maybe cut me a little slack."

That got me a few nods as I left.

With any luck, though, I'd never go back to the Broken Wand. That ambergris smell. That moment of clarity. Maybe that breakthrough would persuade Melifala to train me again.

Only one way to find out.

THE WAY OF MAGIC

THE WORST PART ABOUT LIVING IN A CASTLE WAS THE EXPECTATIONS. Arion had only lived here a week, ever since he'd gotten a position as apprentice to the Royal Wizard, and already the weight of expectations was enough to crush his slender shoulders.

The servants expected him to know his way around without asking. Even though this place was a maze of black stone, full of narrow corridors that twisted and turned on their way, linking huge rooms that all seemed covered in tapestries that told the history of the royal family.

And the history of the Plantagen family went back over a thousand years.

All the rooms smelled like wood smoke. Yes, it was faint enough that most inhabitants of the castle probably didn't even notice it anymore, but Arion had been used to fresh air and lots of sun. Living inside this dark castle just made all the little details stand out all the more.

The smell of wood smoke from the countless fireplaces, all of which seemed to make the huge rooms warm and stuffy, but did nothing to heat the maze of corridors, which all seemed to carry the early winter chill. The dim light, even in the many dining halls and audience chambers.

Enough that Arion felt closed in here, even in the largest rooms.

And it wasn't just the rooms, or getting around. The servants expected Arion to know how Things Had Always Been Done. What the pecking order was, whom to talk to about what. As though he'd lived there most of his life, like they had.

Arion was sure that at least some of that was jealousy of his position.

Arion was younger than most of them, only just getting the first signs of the growth that would one day be an impressive black beard, he was sure. But being the apprentice to the Royal Wizard came with standing beyond anything that any of the other servants could ever hope to achieve. Even though most of them had been born in the castle, or in the town around it, while Arion had been born the fifth son of twelve on a farm that even the villages considered "out of the way."

All the servants had to bow to him. And Arion could see the resentment in their eyes.

The guards were worse. They wouldn't even look at him, much less talk to him. And as far as getting directions to the smithy for resin or the chandler for beeswax and tallow, Arion would have had better luck asking the stone.

And worst of all was his new master. Carnellon the Magnificent. Thin as the oaken staff he carried, with burning orange eyes and wispy white hair. He just cackled at Arion's questions, and said, "Until you learn to read people, my boy, you must read more books."

The books helped. Histories and languages and primers in powers Arion might someday wield. The books were the best part of being an apprentice so far.

Not that the books had much competition. Grinding powders and mixing base elements for potion stock, lighting by hand all the candles that Carnellon could have lit with a gesture. Fetching meals, carrying messages ... both of which meant getting lost.

Just. Like. Now.

Arion was somewhere deep within the bowels of the castle right now, and bowels was how he thought of it. This mission for Carnellon was just one more movement of the castle's bowels, carrying him down the chute.

Parchment. Arion had been sent forth for parchment.

Specific parchment from the Royal Scribe, yes, but still. Carnellon had volumes of unused books, waiting for details of his experiments. Not to mention sheets of vellum and foolscap, waiting for recipes and travel spells and more. In fact, Carnellon had more material for writing than Arion had known existed in the whole of the kingdom, before Carnellon had found him.

That had been the strangest day of Arion's life.

IT HAD STARTED NORMALLY ENOUGH. HE WAS TENDING THE FLOCK AS HE so often did.

Arion had stood on the edge of the mountain valley, shivering under two roughspun cloaks, while the last sheep of the fold came in from their final graze of the season. Only in this little spot of the mountains did the grass stay fresh and unfrozen long enough for that one final graze. It made Arion's family's sheep that much better fortified for the winter.

Arion had never known why their little spot resisted the frost, despite the chill. Not until that day that Carnellon came riding on that black, silent, phantom steed of his. Straight up a section of mountainside he rode, as though the phantom steed were at least half mountain goat. Or perhaps, to the spirit beast, the mountain was flat as any plain.

And Carnellon himself. His burning orange eyes bored into Arion the entire way up the mountainside. Drove the chill straight out of the air, those eyes did.

By the time Carnellon reined up beside Arion, Arion had stopped shivering and stood sweating, in slack-jawed awe.

Carnellon had no time for questions that were not his own. "You, boy. How late in the season does this place resist the frost?"

"A-another week or so, Lord Wizard."

Carnellon looked closer. Arion felt those orange eyes boring straight into his soul.

But the wizard smiled. "Always been this way, hasn't it, my lad? Your whole life?"

"Y-yes, Lord Wizard."

That was the whole conversation. Carnellon rode on past then and straight up to the house of Arion's family. Less than an hour later, Arion sat behind the Royal Wizard on that ghostly horse, trying not to think about how insubstantial it felt between his legs. Trying not to wonder why he'd been chosen, or how the wizard had come to seek him out. Or what Carnellon had offered his parents, in exchange for taking him away from the farm.

So many questions. Not one of them answered yet.

When they'd arrived back at the Royal Castle, the wizard had said only this.

"From this day forward, my boy, you have the right to call me by name, and to ask me any questions about the Art as I teach it to you. I'll never lie to you, but I have the same right to not answer as I see fit, or to withhold my answer until you're ready for it."

But then Carnellon smiled. "Don't worry, my boy. Do as I say and one day it will all make sense. That's the way of magic."

ARION DEVOUTLY HOPED THAT DAY WOULD COME SOON.

He stood now at the junction of eight tunnels. Not a regular junction either. The entrances weren't spaced right of that. Instead, six of the tunnels arrayed out from one side, while only two went the other. And the two, they were broader, and unless Arion was mistaken – which was entirely possible in this place – they had better lighting around their first bends.

The other six were all darker, and Arion thought they were chillier too. As though one or more of them had subtle breezes flowing from them.

One of the stable boys, in a rare moment of camaraderie, had warned Arion that the dank cells beneath the castle seemed to emanate a fell wind.

Arion sniffed at the air, wondering if it was dank enough to count as "fell." It certainly had the smell of wet earth.

He wondered also which way was the path to the Royal Scribe's chambers.

Most of all he wondered which tunnel he'd come through to reach this junction. Just knowing that might help him deduce his next steps.

But they all looked the same. All but the two on the other side. Turning around to get his bearings had done exactly the opposite.

Arion sighed. He could hope that one of those two broader corridors was the path, but what were the chances he could be that lucky?

No. Not lucky. Nothing was ever luck.

That was the first lesson Carnellon had taught him, as they rode to the castle that first day. The only answer Arion had gotten about how Carnellon had known to look for him, could have had any hint that Arion was lucky enough to have a taste of magic about him.

"Nothing is ever luck, my boy. Only the ebb and flow of the forces of this world."

Well, Arion was standing at a choice point. He knew that. And choice points had power all their own. He knew that too. An entire slender volume, *On the Waxing and Waning of Thee Forces*, had seemed to focus on that key point.

Well, if this was a point of power, then Arion should be able to feel the flow of the forces of this world.

So Arion raised his hands above his head, just as high as they could go, which was not so high, because Arion had yet to enjoy any real growth spurts. Then he flexed his wrists so his palms faced out and down. The Pose of the Decider, one of the seven basic poses of the apprentice, and the first one Carnellon expected Arion to master.

Pose assumed, Arion whispered the words that would open his sensations. To control the flow of forces, a would-be wizard must first learn to feel those forces. To understand them.

Arion's senses opened...

Immediately he was overwhelmed. Eight paths from this point, and Eight times eight times eight reasons to take each of them. Some reasons hot with passion – love seeking a tryst, anger seeking release, and more, so many more – others cold with calculation – murder seeking a target, manipulation seeking its victim, and more, so many more – and some a grade of temperature in between.

Each and every reason buffeted at Arion's will, all demanding that he follow them. Fulfill them, as others had sought to do, had failed. Their reasons lingered in the air, the living history of the thousands of years this castle had stood, since before the King's first ancestor set foot into the valley that would one day be the seat of his family's power.

Arion clung to his pose. Body stiff, wrists in place. He forced himself to stay stock still while he gave his mind a moment to adjust to the tumult. Bad as it was, it was no worse than the time Arion had rushed down the mountainside in the middle of that awful winter storm, to save the dozen sheep whose barn had been broken open by the storm. The poor things had run wild, trying to find shelter.

On that day, Arion had managed to focus on the heat of his own body in a way he never had before. From the moment he'd chosen to go after the sheep. Hadn't been ordered by his parents. In fact, they'd tried to stop him. But the heat of desire flooded him, warmed him even in the iciest of winds.

The moment Arion had committed himself to going, nothing would stop him.

And nothing would stop him now.

Arion focused on one thought: he sought the Royal Scribe. That was his mission. His goal. He sought the Royal Scribe, and just as wind and snow had not stopped Arion that horrible day, the wants and needs of those who went before him would not stop him now.

Arion focused on that thought, on his own goal, and his own choice to follow it. For the truth was, he could leave. Carnellon had made that clear. Arion was not bound here. No contract had been signed, no geas placed on his will. Arion could choose to return to his family anytime he wanted, and his family would even get to keep the funds Carnellon had given them.

But then, of course, Arion would never again have the power to become a wizard.

And though the power scared him no little bit, and Carnellon mystified him even more, and the other apprentices and servants seemed to deplore him most of all, Arion was going to succeed.

He would become a wizard.

And that meant he would find the Royal Scribe, even in this maze of corridors and...

...tunnels.

Arion blinked, then blinked again, then blinked a third time, because there was power in the number three.

And on that third blink, Arion was certain. There, among the twists and tugs and yanks and pulls of so many wants and needs, was one desire as clear as crystal, if only as substantial as Carnellon's steed.

That crystal path was Arion's. He was sure of it.

Arion focused all of his will on that crystal path. And he said aloud, "I see my way, and demand my steps to follow it."

Weak, as incantations went, and weaker still for being in his native tongue, but Arion had not mastered any other languages yet. And if there were any spells for finding a Royal Scribe, Arion did not know them.

But he knew his desire. And what was a spell, but desire given shape?

So with those words, Arion lowered his hands. Relaxed his body. Took one step forward.

And almost immediately went the wrong way. For just then, a path of love crossed his way, a path that would lead to the stable girl who smiled shyly whenever Arion had gone to the stables. She had not spoken to him, not even enough to give Arion her name, but Arion had liked that smile. Had thought of it at times, while scrubbing clean this or that thing.

And if Arion followed that path right now, he knew it would lead him to her true. Knew it would be the right time and place to talk to her. Knew that, if nothing else, he could have a friend here in this strange, unwelcoming place.

But if Arion followed that path, he would not find the Royal Scribe.

Arion hesitated, and hesitation invited a thousand thousand other paths to cloud his vision. To buffet at Arion's will, each demanding as much consideration as that one path of love.

Arion's head spun. His lungs worked like those of a panicked sheep. Shivers wracked his body, which now felt the cold even more sharply than before.

Arion forced his arms up once more. But they would not stay. He tried to still his body, but it spun this way and that way despite him, each time at the call of some powerful desire not his own.

Arion did the only thing he could do. He whistled.

He whistled to call himself, the way he had whistled for the sheep. And as the sheep had managed to hear Arion's whistle even in the heart of the worst winter storm in decades, Arion's inner self heard that whistle now.

Not much, but a brief respite. The eye of that emotional storm.

Arion leapt into the Pose of the Decider. Threw everything he had left of his will into finding the Royal Scribe. Pushed until that crystal path came clear.

This time, Arion kept his hands high until he was three steps down the path, then he pulled his hands down and ran.

MORE TWISTS AND TURNS THROUGH NARROW BLACK STONE CORRIDORS, each of them poorly lit, but still Arion held to that crystal path. And with each twist and turn, more and more desires fell away and clearer and clearer came the path ahead of him.

Arion ran faster now. Racing as though he needed to catch a sheep before it reached a cliff's edge. Faster and faster until he ran flat out into a closed door.

SLAM!

Arion bounced off the door, his head pounding like the smith's hammer whenever the smith ignored Arion's request for resin. The corridor seemed to spin, but Arion stayed facing that closed door, even as pain spiked fresh and thudding with each rapid beat of his heart.

Arion stood, hands on his knees, blinking past the pain and trying to slow his breaths, when the door opened. A man opened the door. A man not more than a few years older than Arion, but old enough to have a full blond beard that matched the curls on his head.

"It *was* a knock, master," the man said. "The wizard's new apprentice, I think."

"Yes," Arion panted out. "Me. Wizard's apprentice. Need—"

"Well," a firm, but older voice said, "invite him in already."

The blond man stood aside, and Arion shuffled inside the best lit room he'd been in yet. Even brighter that Carnellon kept his own chambers. Almost blinding after the dim corridors.

It was small, for a room in the castle, but still larger than Arion's family's house. The blond man strode back to his desk, one of two dozen, where the apprentice scribes busied themselves with their work.

Those desks were to Arion's left, below at least a dozen magical lamps. And to Arion's right, a grand desk of mahogany, broader even than Carnellon's, and just as covered with tomes and scrolls.

And looking at Arion from between piles of scrolls, a pair of smiling blue eyes in a wizened brown face.

The Royal Scribe stood and closed the distance to Arion with swift, sure strides. The Royal Scribe moved with the sure certainty of the Lord General, if without the other man's bulk of impressive muscle.

The Royal Scribe was no less impressive in his own way. He wore robes of turquoise, bound by a cord of gold, with soft brown boots that whispered as he walked. He had his hands behind his back.

"So," the Royal Scribe said, stopping in front of Arion, who was only just now catching his breath, though the pain in his skull was still thumping at him. "You are Carnellon's new apprentice, are you? What's your name, boy?"

"Arion, Lord Scribe."

"Very good," the Royal Scribe said with a nod. "I see you understand your titles, at least. And tell me, Arion, why does your master send you to me, when he has no need of a scribe, and probably at least as much parchment as I have, if not more?"

"My master does not share his reasons with me, Lord Scribe, only—"

"I meant," the Royal Scribe said, arching a white eyebrow, "what does he ask you to fetch for him?"

"Begging your pardon, Lord Scribe, but he said that you would know."

The Royal Scribe blinked then, and reached up with one hand to stroke his beardless chin. "Did he now? Tell me, boy, what were his exact words?"

"My lord Carnellon said, 'Arion, I want you to find your way to the Royal Scribe and fetch a parchment for me. He will know which one.'"

"And you found your way, did you?" The Royal Scribe's lips flattened, as though his words tasted bad, but Arion couldn't imagine why.

"Well ... yes, Lord Scribe."

"Evensby." The Royal Scribe waited while the blond man jumped up again from his desk and rushed to the Royal Scribe's side. Then the Royal Scribe said, "Check that corridor. Go as far as two turnings."

The Royal Scribe then smiled at Arion. "We shall see."

Arion tried not to wonder what was going on, so he set himself to counting the scrolls and tomes on the Royal Scribe's desk, then after he had that total, he began on the desks of the apprentices. By the time the blond man had returned, Arion had counted three hundred scrolls and some twenty-three volumes.

"No one, my lord," the blond man said.

"Very well," the Royal Scribe said, and frowned. He returned to his desk, picked up a scroll, then whirled around and said, "Quickly boy, is this the right parchment?"

Arion had no time to think. He had been hoping to get out of here, to get back to Carnellon with the parchment, so Arion could return to his studies. He gave the first answer that leapt to his mind.

"No, Lord Scribe."

The Royal Scribe sighed. "Very well." He picked up a trifolded piece of parchment, sealed with red wax. He handed it to Arion, along with a heavy, velvet pouch.

"Here is the parchment your master wants, as well as the rest of it."

The Royal Scribe turned away. The pouch hung heavy in Arion's hand. He didn't understand. Carnellon had said nothing about a pouch, only the parchment. Arion almost, *almost* asked a question, but he had a bad feeling in the pit of his stomach that told him not to keep questioning those who obviously had no desire to answer. Already the Royal Scribe had gone back to his work, just as his apprentices had.

Arion might as well have not been there.

So Arion turned to leave.

As he closed the Royal Scribe's door behind him, Arion stood in the dark, cramped corridor and realized he didn't know the way back. For a moment, he had the fleeting urge to knock and ask for directions, but just as quickly another idea occurred to him.

Arion took up the Pose of the Decider, and threw his will behind the decision to walk the fastest path back to his master.

Arion found Carnellon not in his own chambers, but in the King's small audience chamber. The King was still young, not yet of his fortieth summer, and had hair the color of flame and, it was said, a temperament to match.

The two men sat at a round oak table, while a pair of servants milled about in the background, one with a jug of wine and the other with a silver tray covered in fruits and cheeses.

Both servants were roundly ignored by their betters. But both the King and the Royal Wizard looked up when Arion stepped into the room.

"How did you get past my guards, boy?" The King said, though his tone sounded more amused than angry.

"I..." Arion quickly fell to his knees and bowed low. "I'm sorry, Your Majesty. I don't know. I—"

"Do stand, Arion," Carnellon said, his voice every bit as amused as the King's. "I told you, Sire, the boy's gift is as strong as my own. He'll be mighty in his day."

"No mean feat," the King said, "I'll grant you, but a thief might have accomplished the same thing."

"A thief would not have known to seek me here. But tell me,

Arion," Carnellon said, without looking away from the King. "Have you the parchment I sent you for?"

"I do, my lord."

"And the rest?"

Arion blinked, but spoke quickly. "I have a pouch as well, my lord."

"You see?" Carnellon asked the King. "Through my own maze he found his way. Even Darian acknowledges it." Then, louder, to Arion, Carnellon said, "Open the scroll and read it, my boy."

Arion broke the wax seal, unrolled the scroll, and read aloud, "Congratulations, you old goat—" Arion slammed his mouth closed and blushed furiously, but Carnellon encouraged him to read on. "You won the bet. Here's your money."

Carnellon smiled at Arion. "The Royal Scribe was once my apprentice. But he failed. Great flare for languages, the lad, but terrible with everything else."

"And you took Darian's bet," the King said, "that you'd never find a better apprentice?"

"No," Carnellon said. "I took his bet that I'd never find an apprentice up to my standards."

Carnellon smiled at Arion again.

"I'd say I have."

Despite the expectations that implied, Arion found himself smiling.

WANDSLINGER

Mitom reined in his piebald gelding and regarded the ruined castle in the distance. Too small for a king or a duke. Had to have belonged to a count or baron before the uprising. Three fallen towers, but from what he could see shading his eyes against the setting sun, the main hall looked mostly intact.

And if he wasn't mistaken, he could see people setting camp. Maybe a dozen or so.

That meant food. Mutton maybe. Or beef.

Just the thought of food was enough to set his stomach gurgling. Two roast rabbits in four days weren't enough for a full-grown man. Especially not the skinny hares running around these green hills west of Lont.

But could he trust these people?

Could he go another day without food?

Mitom checked the holly wand in the sheath on his belt. Wouldn't do to ride up with it drawn, but he wanted it ready. Chances were good that none of them were wizards, but better safe than dead.

No time to waste then. Folks were always a little more eager to meet strangers while the sun was shining. He spurred the gelding forward, racing the sunset.

Down and up the slopes while the north wind promised to bring those thunderheads down from Barracla. Rain within a couple of days. Mitom hoped some of that old baronial hall still had a useful ceiling. As he rode closer, though, he began to doubt that. Looked as though parts of the towers had been melted down by heavy-duty spellfire.

He was halfway up the slope to the encampment — though it was still a final turn out of sight — when someone finally called out to him.

"Close enough."

Man's voice. Ahead and to the left. Mitom reined in his gelding and inhaled sharply through his nose. He could smell the hill grass, and horses, and a few dogs too. But the horses and dogs weren't close. He squinted against the rising gray twilight.

One man. Pointing a crossbow. Crouched on a pile of molten rock big enough to hide a horse and cart. Mitom's fingers itched to draw. One crossbow, he could handle, but no way to tell how many more hid behind that pile of rock.

Nevertheless, Mitom raised his hands.

"Not looking for trouble," he said. "Just looking for food, and hoping you have enough to share."

"No armor." The guard looked over Mitom's red, lace-up shirt and simple brown trousers, but his eyes lingered on the dark, southern skin of Mitom's face before the guard noticed what really concerned him. "That stick on your belt holly?"

"You know what it is."

Rapid footsteps. A runner sent back for instructions.

"What are you doing out here then?"

Mitom sighed. "I talk better on a full stomach."

"Bet you talk better without a bolt in your throat too."

"Anyone *reasonable* to talk to back there?"

"Hold on, hold on." Older voice this time. Used to authority. Respectable amount of gravel to the tone too. Sounded a bit out of breath though. "Let's not start killing each other just yet."

"Your boy's the one making threats," said Mitom. "Haven't even lowered my hands yet."

"You a wizard?"

"You know what I am."

"You here to kill anyone?"

First good question Mitom had heard yet. Maybe the older man, at least, had some smarts to him.

"Nobody's paying me right now, so I can—"

"You swear that." Tone of tempered steel. "You swear it by the red star."

Mitom leaned back in his saddle, blinking in surprise. Even the gelding shuffled a few steps, as though understanding that the old man did indeed know a thing or two.

Mitom was starting to like this guy.

"I swear by the red star, and by the north wind that carries magic: no one is paying me to kill today, and I have not come here with murder in mind." Mitom snorted. "But your boy with the crossbow there is starting to push his luck."

A moment later Mitom saw the guard lower his crossbow.

"Tell you what," said the old man, who remained safely out of sight. "We'll feed you and your horse, and give you a safe place to sleep tonight if you keep that wand in its sleeve and don't mouth off to my people. And if you're looking for work, maybe I'll have some for you. After we get a chance to talk some."

"Sounds fair to me." Mitom lowered his hands. "And I won't start anything. But if your people do, believe I'll finish it."

Mr. Crossbow had the guts to spit when Mitom said that.

Mitom hoped he wouldn't need to make an example out of him.

MITOM ROUNDED THE FINAL CURVE AND FINALLY GOT A GOOD LOOK AT the encampment.

The towers of the old keep were down all right, half-melted the way Mitom expected from spellfire. And the great wooden doors of the main hall had been blasted off their hinges. But the ceiling of that round hall looked secure enough, supported by its solid stone arches, and it was broad enough across that Mitom could have fit his entire home village inside it.

The detritus of a fallen way of life had been swept to the outer edges of the encampment. Out of the way and useless. Broken wood, soiled cloths and tapestries, and the like.

And spread about the cold stone floor of the hall Mitom saw a raiding party.

The old man had more than thirty riders with him, most with crossbows and either pikes or swords. They protected their bodies with good, worked leather and some of them had cobbled together bits of chain or plate armor salvaged from the old knights. A breast-plate here, some chain leggings there. Gave them a motley, but dangerous look.

Most of them had that pale skin and the lighter hair colors that

Mitom was used to seeing north of Edgeton, where the mountains kept the rains from continuing south and clogged up the sky with their clouds. But he saw a few southerners mixed in among the locals.

They were all men, which was the way of things west of Lont. The men went out to do the killing, and the women ran the farms and towns. Stupid, in Mitom's opinion. Some of the deadliest killers he knew were women. And the smartest person he ever met was his old teacher, Thoma. But how the locals picked up the pieces after the uprising was none of his business.

The weapons might have meant a war party. But toward the back, near the horses, a good twenty collies were snuffling and asserting their pack order. No one brought that many dogs to war, and only the desperate would spend their herding dogs that way.

The men were grouped in tens, each with a stewpot over a fire, while one cook roasted a big ewe over a single, larger fire in the center of the camp. Looked like they were burning what was left of the old noble's tables.

But the smell was heaven to Mitom. The roasting sheep and the stewing carrots and peas and potatoes made his stomach gurgle its anticipation so loudly that the pale old man chuckled as he walked up, a young groom with buck teeth by his side.

No man that wrinkled and white haired should have been out leading a raiding party. Down in the south, people would have given him the title of "elder" and braided his long hair and beard. He'd have sat on a council, not rode forth with leather on his frame and a sword at his side. Even if he did look like he could cleave a man's head from his body in one swing.

"You'll have to trust us with your horse if you want to eat our food."

Mitom raised an eyebrow at the old man, but said nothing as he slid down from the saddle and patted the gelding for reassurance. But before he handed his reins to the groom he made a show of digging a soft woolen blanket out of his saddlebag — and displaying the five-pointed protection star graven on the inside of the leather.

"None of my people are stupid enough to try to rob a man who carries holly."

Mitom let the bag fall closed as though he only meant to pull out a blanket.

The old man sighed and shook one finger in the air. Mitom saw at least a half-dozen men from the different groupings raise their already-loaded crossbows. Mitom put his back to the gelding and let his fingers play near his wand's sleeve, knees bent and ready and black eyes swearing the old man would die before he did.

"Just a precaution," said the old man, raising his hands. "You need to turn out your pockets, shake out your boots and show us everything in those saddlebags. Holly is one thing. But if you're carrying onyx..."

Onyx, the favored weapon of nobles. The key to all mind magic.

Mitom spat.

"You think I'd be standing here half-starved if I was an onyxhead?"

"I think I don't even know your name, much less why you're riding alone. And yes, if you were caught using onyx, you might just be half-starved and in the middle of nowhere, desperate for a little of our food."

"Name's Mitom. I got run out of Lont 'cause I'm too good at cards. Wouldn't believe I wasn't cheating, and I wasn't willing to kill a man for being a sore loser."

The old man gave Mitom a look, Mitom knew that this old man had made hard decisions all his life. Probably fought in the uprising. Probably killed an onyxhead or two in his day.

A look that said he was ready to kill Mitom, just to be sure.

And the old man had a lot of crossbows backing his play.

"All right," said Mitom. "But that cook of yours better not try to short me on the mutton. And I expect some ale or beer to wash it down."

Mitom turned and started taking the saddlebags off his gelding. Once some of these locals got a look at just how much Mitom had won at cards before Lont ran him out of town, they might be willing to find out just how fast a draw Mitom was. Might be gambling that the protective spells on his saddlebags wouldn't be worth much once Mitom was dead.

And if Mitom had to start killing, this night would get real unpleasant.

"We're raiding the O'Korri stead," said the old man, whose name Mitom now knew to be Willad.

The two of them were sitting together, along with the guard who spat at Mitom earlier. A guard named Tinak, who kept his hand near the dagger on his belt through the whole conversation. Mitom didn't mind. The Willad never said Mitom couldn't pull the dagger out of his tall leather boots and gut the fool.

Still, might have been a bad move, sitting near the big roasting fire, surrounded by more than thirty men who were likely to take Tinak's part of any quarrel with the outsider.

Besides, the fire was warm, and crackled pleasantly as it worked its way through the hacked-apart bits of old oak benches. And the smell of the roast ewe lingered in Mitom's nose much as its taste lingered on his tongue. Had to have been seasoned with peppercorns and rosemary. Even the sounds of the other raiders talking and joking to one another gave the air a feel of downright conviviality.

If the price of enjoying the fire, the food, and the company was listening to the occasional slight or implication from Tinak, well, Mitom could pay it and still have patience left over.

"The O'Korris stole ten of my calves last week. Fresh borns they were. Barely had their legs under them, and not yet tough enough to brand." Willad shook his head. "But I know those markings, and Tinak here saw at least three of them when I sent some of the boys to investigate."

"At least three," said Tinak. "Maybe five. Couldn't get close enough to be sure."

Willad might have known his own calves on sight, but Mitom had his doubts about Tinak. In his most diplomatic moment of the month, Mitom chose not to say this.

"So now you want to steal them back?"

"Plus a few more as a lesson. O'Korri needs to know we won't sit still for this."

And, of course, the one raid would lead to another and then another, until they gave up the raids and went to war. And wars were usually when people hired men like Mitom.

And even the money in Mitom's saddlebag wouldn't last forever.

"So you figure riding with me will make a bigger statement than just your crossbows and such."

"Haven't had a," — Willad hesitated over his choice of words — "man like you through here in some time. You ride with us tomorrow and that should encourage O'Korri to accept our raid as the final statement in the matter."

"Won't be cheap." Especially after the indignity of that search earlier. "You have that kind of ready coin?"

"How do we know that's not just a stick?" said Tinak. "Maybe he cut if off a holly bush himself and carries it for show."

Willad froze.

"For all the ritual that's been done over it, it *is* just a stick," said Mitom, his voice quiet. "It's the man carrying it you ought to be afraid of. And that man is getting tired of listening to you."

"Go make sure Mitom's horse has good shoes," said Willad. "And don't get any funny ideas, because I'll check it myself later."

Tinak looked back and forth between Mitom and Willad, then scoffed and jumped to his feet so he could stomp off properly.

"Nephew?" said Mitom.

"Grandson."

"I worry about the future of your name."

"Then ride with me tomorrow. I'm sure we can come to an arrangement."

They haggled over the price for the better part of an hour. But in the end, Mitom was satisfied with the sum. Even if the old man could only give him half up front.

But Mitom had a bad feeling about the raid all the same. Something about Willad's tone when he talked about O'Korri. Made it sound like this wasn't just about cattle...

Maybe Mitom should have asked for more money after all.

———

When dawn broke over the eastern hills the next morning, Mitom rode north into the teeth of the wind at the head of the raiding party, on Willad's right hand. Tinak rode on Willad's left hand, and Willad gave his grandson lessons in raiding and leading a battle as they crossed the green rolling hills.

Not much of a dawn, in Mitom's opinion. It should have brought warm rays to stave off the last of the night's chill. But instead the sun barely crested the hills before it got caught up in more of those dark gray thunderheads coming down with the wind from Barracla in the north.

Turned the dawn gray and combined with the wind to chill away even the memory of last night's pleasant fire. Made the cold breakfast stew sit heavier in Mitom's belly.

Fortunately, that old ruin had proven an excellent staging area. They'd barely been riding an hour when Willad called a slowdown just short of a series of rolling hills with a triangular formation of white stone atop the tallest.

A third of the party broke off, with the collies. They rode to take up a position to the west.

"Once more," said Willad, as much to Tinak as to Mitom. "The herders should be in place before we reach the pens. The breakers" — Willad gestured at another third of his group, who had axes as well as their other weapons — "get the pens open and drive the cattle to the meet-up point. The rest of us hit the O'Korris hard and give the others time to work.

"Clear?"

Mitom merely nodded, but Tinak barked "Willad!" as though the family name was his battle cry.

"Try not to warn the whole countryside before we reach our objective," said Willad, with more patience than Mitom would have shown the fool.

Willad started the horses forward at a trot, but then built it to a gallop before they reached the hills. More than twenty horses pounding their way up the green grass. The riders had pikes or swords or bows at the ready, all save Mitom who would not draw his wand until the time came to use it. Up the hills the rode like fury.

But they were not alone.

Before they reached the top, riders crested the hills. Riders with crossbows and swords and battleaxes and pikes.

More than twice as many as old Willad brought to the raid.

Mitom glanced at the old man. Willad would have only a moment to make his decision. Mitom didn't like the odds, but he'd fought on the wrong side of bad odds before.

But Willad called the halt. No more than twenty yards separated the raiders from the thoroughly unsurprised O'Korris. The O'Korris had numbers on their side, and high ground. And by calling the halt, Willad had denied his men even the momentum of their charge.

But the old man's eyes were fixed on the center of the host. A woman. A young woman. Pretty in that northern way, with smooth pale skin and lustrous dark hair. She wore dark brown leathers, but not as though she were used to armor.

A woman who was smiling at Tinak. And Tinak was smiling back.

"Sorry, grandfather," said Tinak, though nothing of apology could be heard in his tone, "but I knew you would never accept my desire to marry Ulloi here. And if I can't join our families properly, at least I can join our lands the hard way."

"I can think of a reason that won't work out," said Mitom, his fingers playing near the sheath of his wand. He looked over at Willad for permission, but Willad's attention was entirely on Tinak. The old man might not have even heard Mitom speak.

"Fool," said Willad, and Mitom heard honest sorrow in the old man's voice. "O'Korri is using you, the way she tried to use me when I was your age. She'll never let this girl marry you."

"You never trusted me!" shouted Tinak. "You never believed that I could handle myself. That I could make my own decisions. But I'm the one calling the shots now. And I—"

Tinak's words were interrupted by a crossbow bolt to the chest, ordered by a pointing gesture of Ulloi.

"However did you tolerate his whining?" asked Ulloi, but Mitom could barely hear her words over the anguished cry of Willad, who leapt down from his horse and ran to catch his falling, dying grandson. The host of Willad's men rumbled with cries and grumblings.

The old man and his grandson shared whispered words then, but Mitom could not hear them. His eyes were watching Ulloi. And she finally seemed to notice him.

"Well, a wandslinger. And a southerner at that. And here Tinak assured me just two days ago that none of your kind had ridden through Willad lands since before this past winter." She shook her head. "Whatever he's paying you, I'll double it to forsake him."

"That's not how this works," said Mitom.

"Oh, I'm not asking you to kill a former employer." She made the words sound dull. As though she were bored by a debate about whether or not the pattern of a cow's coat affected the flavor of its meat. "You don't even need to raise your weapon. Just ride over here next to me. Once I've settled matters with Willad, we can ride back to the house and I'll get you your money."

"Kill her," said Willad, voice hoarse and face stained with tears, his dying grandson still coughing in his arms. "Kill her and I'll double your pay myself."

"Then I'll double that," said Ulloi. "Honestly, Willad, you're not in much of a position to haggle." She looked up at Mitom. "And I have no doubt that you could kill me faster with that twig than my men could kill you with their bolts. So. Southerner. Will you take my money so you and I can both get out of this alive?"

Tinak shuddered then, and died. Mitom knew better than to look at Willad. Willad had given his order. No doubt he expected Mitom to follow it, even if it meant getting shot down by fifty crossbows a moment later.

But Mitom had not lived this long by being stupid.

He clucked his tongue at his piebald gelding, and trotted across the gap until he was next to Ulloi.

"Coward!" screamed Willad. "Useless fop. You're worse than a noble."

But Mitom sat astride his horse and weathered the tirade. Ulloi smiled at Willad through his continued bursts of invective until she tired of that too.

"This is why you men are unfit to rule," she said "You're all too emotional. That boy was a waste of space. And to think I let him kiss me." She shuddered. "No, Willad, I'm afraid that even if Grandmother approved — and you're quite right, she wouldn't — I would never have consented to marry Tinak. He had nothing to interest me beyond your land.

"And speaking of that land." Ulloi stretched her back straighter and looked as far toward the horizon as she could see in the gray morning light. "I don't want to kill you, Willad. I don't even want to kill your men."

She tilted her head pensively. "I *did* want to kill Tinak, but honestly once you've calmed down you'll see that I've done you a favor there. He would have made a terrible heir for you."

"I will see you dead," said Willad, as though his gaze alone could do the job. "And for killing my grandson I will spit on your corpse before I feed it to my dogs."

"Yes, well," said Ulloi, "I think we can all agree that you won't do that *today*." She gestured to her superior numbers. "So let's talk about what today means to our families. Now for the crimes of false accusation and attempted cattle theft, I think proper recompense would be ... shall we say ... the grazing lands between here and the river Nolt?"

Mitom knew that the river Nolt was a good three days south of the hill they spoke on.

Willad's voice came rough and low, and his glare still promised Ulloi evil.

"Tinak was not the only witness to your theft."

"The only witness of your blood, so the only witness whose opinion—"

The rest of Ulloi's words were cut off when Mitom grabbed her arm and yanked her down with him between their horses while his free hand grabbed both sets of reins.

THE RAIDERS AND DEFENDERS BUZZED WITH HOPE AND OUTRAGE, respectively. Mitom huddled there between his piebald gelding and Ulloi's chestnut stallion, both nickering. Mitom had their reins in one hand and his wand in the other, with its holly tip in the center of her leather breastplate.

"Dismiss your men," he said.

"They'll kill you before you—"

"They can't get a clear shot with us between these horses, and your life is shrinking by the second. Dismiss your men."

Ulloi's eyes widened, panic in the whites around their dark blue. No doubt she saw her own death in Mitom's eyes.

"Ba... Back to the barn," she said, but the words weren't much above a whisper.

Mitom scowled.

"Back to the barn," she yelled, though each word shook. "Now. All of you."

Her men hesitated.

"Do it now!"

That finally seemed to get through to them. They turned to ride off, though Mitom noted that nearly half of her men tried to angle their crossbows for a clear shot as they rode. But Mitom kept the two steeds between his body and their bolts.

"Tell grandmother I'll be home soon," Ulloi called out to her retreating men, and Mitom heard hope in her voice. Saw it in her eyes as she searched his.

But Mitom promised nothing.

Once the men were out of comfortable firing range, Mitom

turned his attention back to Willad, who still knelt on the grass, the dead Tinak in his arms. Confusion in his eyes though.

That, Mitom would answer.

"I told her," he said. "That isn't how this works. I'm not a mercenary." He smiled at his prisoner. "But if she wants to then invite me inside her guard, more the fool her."

Ulloi composed herself, wiped away the initial tears that fear had squeezed out before she reasserted control. She stood before them tall and proud and unapologetic.

"Very well, Willad. I am your prisoner. But you know I am a valuable prisoner. My grandmother would pay—"

"I said kill her," said Willad.

Mitom made it quick. Burnt her to ash with green fire in less time than it would have taken her to finish her final sentence.

"The O'Korris will come after you for that," he said.

"I haven't finished with them. There's still the matter of my cattle."

"I'll wait for you at the meet-up point," said Mitom, mounting his horse.

"But the raid," said Willad.

"You already offered me double to kill Ulloi. Can you afford to pay me for the raid on top of it?"

"Fine," Willad spat. But then he had a thought. "But you're taking Tinak's body with you."

Mitom grimaced. Lugging corpses now.

The things he had to do to survive up here in the north.

SHADOW OF A CURSE

APPLES WEREN'T SUPPOSED TO FLOAT IN THE AIR. EVERYONE KNEW THAT. If an apple slipped from the edge of a barmaid's tray, it was supposed to fall down to bounce on the weathered oak of the floor. It wasn't supposed to stop itself in mid-air, catching the immediate attention of a half-dozen of the tavern's revelers in the process.

It wasn't supposed to stop all conversation at the three nearest bench tables while mercenaries and tradesmen and farmers alike turned their attention to stare at the sweet green globe the size of a man's fist, twisting in the air limned in a golden sheen.

But the apple did just that. Perhaps the first time in the history of the Green Goose tavern that a single apple had drawn the attention of hungry men and women from their feast on the night's roast boar and snap peas, to say nothing of the mugs of fine beer forgotten in so many hands.

An apple floated in mid-air. Magic. More magic than most of them would see in a lifetime.

More magic than Asi should have spent for no better reason than to turn a pretty barmaid's expression from irritation to awestruck wonder. But only a year past his own apprenticeship, Asi still believed that wonder alone was worth the cost of a little magic.

And the barmaid was very pretty. Long black hair with the slight curve of an arrow's flight. That northern tilt to her brown eyes alongside the slender build of a woman who had never carried an axe. Her complexion a rich brown kissed by lemons rather than snowy, and her undyed cotton dress hung barely past her knees.

So different from the women of Asi's icy homeland.

Asi raised his gold-limned left hand and the apple lifted up through the air to float before the barmaid's face. She laughed with glee as she touched the apple. It fell into her hand as the sheen of gold vanished from around it and around Asi's hand. She smiled wide-eyed at Asi, and he shared that smile before the moment was ruined.

"Varlock."

Asi didn't see who spoke the title, but no sooner had someone uttered it than the word spread through the tavern like a hushed echo, with varying degrees of accent and inebriation. He was surprised they knew the word here, though perhaps they knew it only by rumor.

Dozens of eyes turned toward him. Most of them belonging to locals like the barmaid. Other eyes from wanderers and mercenaries and traders from the southern wastes or the western archipelago. Some of them reached for coin purses. Others narrowed their eyes in suspicion. But a few reached for weapons. Just in case.

Eight long bench tables in the room, all full, and all with attention turning Asi's way. He felt them scrutinize his frost-white skin and long, sun pale hair. Marks of his homeland as true as his gray wolf cloak or – apparently – the red shirt he wore with his leather trousers.

So much attention made him glance past the bench tables to the corners. Assessing the room again. Another round table in each corner, plus the two-countered bar running like a spike down the center, from the back of the common room to the mid-point. The doors into the kitchen were behind the bar. A large stone hearth in each long wall, and stairs at the back leading to rooms upstairs.

Asi sat alone at a round table. Near to the front door, but all the way across the tavern from those stairs. He had a room waiting for him, if he still got to use it. And he had yet to enjoy his own dinner.

With every eye in the tavern on him now, and his title on the lips of every patron, Asi admonished himself to leave the local women alone next time.

But then he thought of the barmaid's smile, and knew he would do the same thing the next time. And the time after that.

One of the locals was the first to gather his courage. An older man, in an undyed linen tunic and pants with a rope belt, which appeared to be the local fashion. He had the slight bow to his back that came from a life of field work, and a wispy white beard dripping down from his chin like a melting icicle.

"Varlock," he said, with a smoother bow than Asi expected. And his voice sounded strong, certain. Perhaps the local farmers did more talking than back home. "I—"

"Before you begin..." said Asi, holding up a hand, and the little old man stilled his mouth and waited patiently for Asi to speak. "I need you all to hear this. Those of my order are not 'for hire' like the kanuas of the archipelago or the sorcerers of the wastes. I am a varlock. I will sit and See for this town if you wish, but I must be fed and lodged by the town, and not my own coin. And each seeker will receive an answer only as fair and valuable as the offering made."

Formal phrasing, used by every varlock. Some assumed it meant only the rich could afford a Seeing. In truth, it meant the more personally important the question, the more personally important the offering must be to receive a meaningful answer.

"I am San," the old man said. "And I sit on the council for this, the township of Thir. And we do not need you to See for us, though of course we appreciate the offer."

Several in the crowd groaned at that and a few uttered protests, but not loudly. They must indeed have known the reputation of the varlocks, for they seemed to know that if a community leader said there would be no Seeing, no individual had the right to ask for one.

Perhaps a floating apple was not the most magic these locals would see in their lifetime after all.

"But we do have need of a varlock," San said loudly over the grumbles. "It is said that varlocks are curse breakers. And there is a curse on our lands."

Asi felt his stomach suggest that he was not so hungry as he'd thought. Why did he have to show off? He could have ridden out of this little town in the morning and never again given it a moment's thought. He would not have had to risk his life, his magic and at least one ninth part of his soul against the source of a land curse.

But then he looked at the barmaid and her evident interest in the mysterious varlock talking to a council member.

And Asi knew. He would do it again the same way the next time, assuming he survived.

After all, what was life without a little risk and the occasional interest of a pretty girl?

Asi invited San to join him at the table and San told the barmaid – whose name was Kyo – that the varlock's meal would be paid for by the town tonight, and that she should bring the best beer with dinner, and brandy with cherries and sweet apples for dessert.

Though they sat alone in the corner, Asi noticed that the rest of the tavern conversation had hushed, if not in fact lulled. It seemed that everyone was curious to listen in on what the councilor had to say. Curious enough that Asi could hear the fires on both sides of the room crackle and pop their spruce logs, and even the pouring of the master of the house at the bar.

Asi settled back into his simple chair and regarded San with raised eyebrows. The councilman smiled.

"This cannot be the first time you have discussed business in front of a crowd."

"It's the first time I've been in a town this small that knew the rules and expectations of dealing with varlocks." Asi tilted his head. "At least, a town that does not see snowfall for at least half the year."

"There is a tall woman who comes through once a year and Sees for us. She stands about your height with hair as red as sunset. She wears a gray wolf cloak the twin of yours."

"Rika?" Asi sat forward, both elbows on the rough wood of the table and his entire attention on San, who seemed pleased that Asi knew the name. "*Rika* has Seen for you?"

"She has done other things for us as well."

Beneath his breath, Asi uttered a small prayer of thanks that San had refused a Seeing. If Rika was all they knew of varlocks here, they would have very high expectations for Asi's work...

San smiled, and relaxation seemed to spread from the old man's eyes down his beard and all through his body.

"Good," said San. "Humility. I wondered."

Humility. Asi almost laughed. Saying his own power was nothing to Rika's was like saying a snowball was nothing to an avalanche.

"If Rika can't break the curse—"

"She has not been here since the curse was laid, and if we wait for her we will all be dead before she arrives."

"All of you?" Asi sat back in his chair, so struck by the councilman's statement that he failed to give Kyo so much as a flirtatious look when she filled his mug with beer. "But most curses affect one person. One family. One farm. One business. That is their nature."

"And we are one town." San shrugged. "One town with our cattle and sheep dying and our horses dead already. One town paying foreign hunters to kill boars while we fight to save our livestock. I don't know how we have angered such a powerful witch, but we have. And she blames the whole of our community."

Asi shook his head.

"No witch could do this. A varlock could do it, if powerful enough..." Asi closed his eyes. "You swear to me on your town's children that you have not angered Rika?"

"I swear to you on our children and on the children I hope they live to bear, here in Thir we treat Rika as a treasured aunt. No door is closed to her. No meal or bed denied her. Offerings left for her when she is not looking. Her money spurned when offered. Our people would shed their blood for her."

Asi nodded slowly. If he had any lingering doubts, those words assuaged them. The goal of a varlock was not power or glory, but community. That Rika came through annually, and that Thir treated her properly, meant that this was not merely someplace Rika came to See. This was a place she could call home. And no other varlock would *dare* to curse a place *Rika* called home.

Yet something had. Something that could spread a curse past the bonds of family and property to community itself. And if not a varlock, then that meant more power than anything Asi had faced before.

Fear twitched in his stomach, clenched someplace lower. This was Asi's first trip down from the frozen east. He wished to do nothing more than ride for the coast and visit the archipelago, where the sea was said to flow as warm as blood and they shared fruits the like of which Asi had never tasted.

But this was a community in crisis. And though the source of such a curse may well have been beyond his means to defeat, Asi could no more walk away from their troubles than he could fail to return each year to the village that bore him, and treat its woes.

And so Asi swallowed a sigh and said the formal words of a varlock to a community leader he is promising to aid.

"I am sorry to hear of your troubles, uncle. Tell me everything so I know how to help."

San leaned forward and clasped Asi's hand. And then he told the tale. Others from nearby tables stood to offer insights and other viewpoints. Some of the wanderers left, uncomfortable, as the locals laid bare their troubles. And Asi was certain he could see some of the merchants and traders looking for angles to improve their profits.

That was reason enough to interrupt the tales of cows and sheep wasting away even as they ate and drank their normal share of fodder and water. Of pear trees stunting at the blossom, and the apple and cherry trees that seemed to be following suit. Of farmland that drank deep the rains, yet thirsted for more.

Asi stood amid the recitations, stopping a farmer mid-sentence.

"A warning," Asi said, "to those who trade and sell. Rika may not be here, but I am varlock enough to deal with any who would exploit this curse. Do *not* let me hear of raised prices or unreasonable demands."

And ignoring the grumbles and furtive looks among merchants and mercenaries, Asi sat and listened to every one of the complaints while the problem grew and grew in his own mind. Curses dealt with health, or livestock, or crops, or land. They did not deal with health *and* livestock *and* crops *and* land. Not even a varlock's curse did so many things at once. A varlock's curse would pick a single path to cut through a community and slice it to ribbons in a fortnight.

But this was different. This was slow, thorough, and ugly.

And Asi had no idea what was causing it.

***

ASI WOKE IN THE MORNING ON THE INNKEEPER'S FINEST FEATHER BED, entwined in the limbs of Kyo. He kissed her as she awoke, tender, to savor her sweetness just a little longer before going out to face this town's need.

Kyo made a small sound, squeezed her eyes closed, and tried to pull him back down to sleep. But much as he might have desired to join her, Asi could not permit that. If he lay back down with Kyo, he knew he would not leave that bed until the sun was high in the sky, and he needed to see the afflicted area by the first rays of the dawn.

So he kissed her again, and he stroked her cheek to soothe her. And once her brown eyes had fluttered closed and her breaths grown deeper, Asi leaned down to enjoy her warm scent that reminded him of nutmeg.

Then he placed his hand on the center of her naked chest, and muttered a half-Seeing, half-blessing.

"When the rays of the longest day begin to fade, they shall shine last upon he who is your truest love. You shall see that truth in one another's eyes, and shall be happy together through all the trials of life."

And just for a moment, a reddish glow flowed from Asi's chest and down his arm to spread across Kyo's body. When it faded, she smiled in her sleep.

The night before Kyo might been willing to share Asi's bed anyway, because he was handsome and mysterious. But once Asi agreed to aid the community of Thir with all his skill as a varlock, no bed would be denied him and he would leave every lover blessed.

Asi left his cloak behind in the room, and donned a shirt of sky blue over his leather pants and heavy leather boots. He broke his fast on the apple and small wedge of sharp yellow cheese that had been left on a plate for him, and examined the town in the pre-dawn as he walked north along the smooth main road toward the first farm harmed by the curse.

Rika must have been coming here for years. Asi could see the signs of a strong community. A community that helped its own.

The houses all began small, but steady, and spaced widely enough to expand back and out as families grew. And every house in the town itself looked solid. Good woods in the construction and sealed against rain, trued angles, and shingled roofs. No family had suffered because of a father or mother's poor fortune or ineptitude with a hammer.

Even now he could hear the families rising to begin their days. Calling to each other, or to their livestock. Those latter cries sounding plaintive in Asi's ears, as though they hoped to persuade their animals to live through the sheer power of love and need.

Multiple wells. Large in the center of town, and smaller secondary wells spaced every few hundred steps. This was a community that pulled together despite a gentle climate and forgiving soil that made all too many communities selfish.

No wonder Rika felt home here.

As Asi reached the farms north of town, he saw that the family markings here and there on the fences had been redone two or three times. Territory disputes at the edge of town? Interesting. Perhaps Thir was not so harmonious as Asi had thought.

Asi considered that as he reached the Etu farm, the farthest out from town center. If this town's harmony had begun to fray at the edges, then along the edges Asi might find the answers to this curse.

If so, this was where he would learn the truth.

Asi took up the proper position, right knee pressed against the earth just outside the fence of the Etu farm. Back straight and eyes level with the distant mountains of the horizon. Right hand out to the side, palm up. Left hand out to the side, palm down.

In the language of his homeland, he chanted, "Far Farer grant me a grain of your Sight. Show me what hides between darkness and light."

The first ray of sunshine crested the mountain peaks and shone down across the valley onto the farm.

Asi saw the land cracked drier than the southern sandy wastes. He saw desperate carrion birds squabbling over the scraps of corpses too desiccated to feed even one of them. Buildings fallen. Crops blackened.

Asi saw a land drained dry of life.

Then the moment passed, and Asi saw the Etu farm as it was rather than as it would be. Sickened, not dead. Not yet.

But one element still remained from what the Far Farer showed Asi. A wispy trail like a hint of black smoke, trailing north of town toward a dense forest a half-day distant.

Asi would need his horse.

ASI WAS OBLIGED TO REFUSE HELP THREE TIMES BEFORE THE TOWNSFOLK would let him ride forth alone to deal with the threat. They were strong men and women, and many of them had fought in defense of their own before. Some could even wield a sword as handily as an axe or hoe.

But Asi knew they would be useless against the thing that had cursed their town. True, weapons might have been able to harm, or even defeat it. Asi would not know that for certain until he traced that smoky trail to its source and determined exactly what manner of threat he faced.

But even if they could kill it, they would not be able to help Asi. Worse, they might hinder his progress. Some curses could only be broken while the curser lived. Killing the curser merely ensured that the spell ran its course.

The ways and varieties of magic were many, and no one, not even Rika, could claim to know them all. It was the calling of the varlock to puzzle through their secrets in service to others. So he accepted the one thing he needed – a scrap of parchment bearing the council's seal – and rode off on his own to face the threat.

To reach the thick, supposedly uninhabited forest, Asi had to leave the road where it bent west. The road would wind its way across the river Shem, heading for the nearest city. Or at least the nearest lord. Whichever way the locals ran things.

But even without a boundary marker, Asi knew the moment his chestnut palomino Ulf passed beyond the northern edge of the Etu farm. Yellowing grass grew greener, had more spring to it. The soil beneath was richer, darker, even softer than the hardening dryness of the farmlands behind him. The air smelled sweeter here, fresher. As though rain had been no more than three days past. The heat of the morning sunlight felt heartening on Asi's skin, rather than suggesting an itch that could not *quite* be felt.

Ulf's steps lightened as well, as though merely passing through Thir had weighed on the poor horse.

And so Asi spurred Ulf to a swift trot, determined to enter the distant forest before the sun reached its apex.

He reached the outlying ash trees perhaps an hour before high sun.

Asi dismounted, and stood before Ulf. He stroked the horse's blond mane, and spoke into his soft brown eyes. "Await me here, my friend. If you must flee a threat, follow the road west. I will find you. Do not return to Thir without me."

Asi sighed. "If I do not return by nightfall, go home."

A varlock's horse returning without the varlock was rare, and always merited investigation. If Asi died today, Ulf would carry the warning. Another would return to finish what Asi started. Perhaps Rika herself.

Ulf neighed an objection.

"Very well then," said Asi. "Dawn." Asi held up a warning finger. "I mean it. If I do not return by dawn, consider me lost. Do not tarry in danger, my friend."

Ulf snorted and jerked his head away. He took three firm steps along the tree line, glanced back at Asi, then pointedly began munching on grass.

"I don't like it either," said Asi. "But there are no roads through this forest, and I won't have you breaking an ankle. I'll be back by dawn, if I return at all."

Ulf munched some more grass, which was about all the agreement Asi could expect.

Asi turned back to the forest. He plucked three leaves from the nearest ash tree and one leaf from each of three small plants that formed the underbrush. He rooted around in the bushes, and among the twigs and fallen leaves until he had a feather from one of the local jays – blue – and a tuft of red fox fur.

He gathered all these things in his left hand, placed his right hand over them, not touching. Blue power flared from his solar plexus, then up his chest and down his arms to coalesce in his hands, lighting his gathered materials.

In the tongue of his native land, he whispered, "Wights and spirits, hear me. You who grow, who run, who fly. You who form this place, and you who call it home. Hear me. You who bear no evil, hear me. I seek a shadow hiding among you. I seek a darkness that poisons the land. I seek a foulness that corrodes animal and human alike. Let me be as one of you, for a time. Let me hunt as one of you, for a time. Let me call this place home, for a time. Help me root out this foulness, and I shall leave your home a better place than I found it."

The blue power faded. Asi moved his right hand aside. The leaves, the feather and the fur were gone from his left hand. In their place lay a single green feather, small and simple as the pinion of a sparrow.

Asi raised the feather reverently and whispered, "Thank you."

He placed the feather behind his right ear and started into the forest.

It was as though the forest opened wide before him. Every sight, every sound, every smell came to him, but all came filtered. The trees and underbrush were as background to the smoky trail he followed. He heard the birdsong, the chatter of squirrels, the cracking and rustling of countless animals going about their business, unconcerned about the human who was – for a time – as one of them. But those sounds were muffled as his ears strained for the unnatural, although, as yet, he heard nothing.

And the smells of the forest, the musk of the animals and the damp decay of recent rain, those hung back as well. No more prominent than his tongue's memory of the apples and sharp yellow cheese, eaten hours ago.

Overriding all these things, Asi could smell a whiff of corruption.

As of a wound that had begun to fester, but not yet gained the sickly sweetness of gangrene.

Only a hint, but it lay in the same direction as the smoky trail led him.

Surefooted and confident as any woodland creature, Asi began to run.

THE TRAIL LED ASI DEEP INTO THE FOREST. HE CROSSED SMALL HILLS and leapt creeks and streams, while all around him animals went about their day, unconcerned about his presence. If only he could have spared the attention to revel in this harmony. But he kept his focus on the thin, smoky trail, and on the thing that was cursing the township of Thir.

Between trees he followed it. Through bushes and across ditches, his attention never flagging.

Finally, the smoky trail dipped down to a pool.

The pool wasn't in a clearing. Ashes and beeches grew right up to its edge, and Asi could see their roots and underbrush dipping down as though expecting solid ground. Above, the canopy grew thick, and if the forest had not welcomed Asi, his eyes would have seen little. If anything.

But the forest did welcome Asi after his petition, and Asi could see the chunk of granite overhanging the pool, like a great gray diver preparing to plunge. It stood taller than Asi, and wider than a cart.

Asi could also see that this pool wasn't fed by streams. Nor rainwater, not under so thick a canopy. If the pool, itself, were natural, it would have to have been fed by an underground spring.

But this pool wasn't natural. No animals came here to drink. Asi could see no tracks, smell no spoor nor musk. In fact, he smelled little except for the rank corruption, strong enough now to turn his stomach and threaten to bring back up that sharp yellow cheese.

Asi pulled out the scrap of parchment bearing the seal of the council. He held it high, and a golden glow of power limned himself and the parchment as he spoke.

"I have come. I name myself protector of Thir. I name myself guardian of this forest. I name myself breaker of your curse. My name is Asi Kholsson, and I have come. Step forth and give answer."

The rock began to shift and bend, and beneath it the pool rushed up in a pillar of water. Rock flowed as though molten and began to twist and dance with the water, swirling together. Spiraling up, up, up all the way to the canopy some two dozen feet overhead, before crashing back down into a single shape.

A gray stone serpent, with watery blue eyes that rippled. Its body was thicker than Ulf, and long as one of the trees around it. The serpent coiled where the pool had been, head weaving back and forth, high in the air, as its hood flared out. Stone fangs glistened with water or poison.

Poison. Of course.

"What are you?" said Asi. This creature was like nothing they had back home.

"Varrr-loch," it rasped, and for a horrible moment Asi thought it was saying that it was once a varlock. But as it continued, Asi realized it was addressing him by a title he never gave it. Fortunately, it's voice became easier to understand as it continued. "Deny Thir. It is dead already. Leave this place. And live."

"If you know I am a varlock," said Asi, tucking the parchment back into his belt, "you know I won't. You *do* know of varlocks, don't you? That's why you act now. You fear Rika."

"You are no Rika."

"No, but that does tell me you can be killed." Asi smiled. "Break your curse and leave. Do these things and you will live."

Something that big should not have been fast.

It struck. Great dripping fangs plunged for Asi's chest.

Asi grabbed the stone mouth. Held it wide open, while the mouth bore him down. Onto his back among the twigs and fallen leaves.

Breath like rotted meat, practically a poison of its own. But the inside of the mouth was stone, not meat. No proper gullet then.

And that gave Asi an idea.

First, he channeled his connection to Thir into a golden glow of power and spent that glow in a single kick. He snapped off one of those poison fangs. Sent it flying.

The creature roared anger and pain. Pulled back for another strike.

Asi dove into the mouth. Beside the snapping fang he went, straight down the creature's throat. He could feel it rising high. Maybe trying to swallow. Maybe trying to expel him. But a creature that does not eat cannot really...

The inside of its throat began to shift. Grew slippery. Oily. Began to slide Asi down toward its center. Asi knew what would follow then. Another shift of shape, and then it would begin to crush him as surely as any digestive tract.

But Asi never planned on giving it the chance.

Green power spread from Asi's heart to envelope him, shining out into the glittery throat of the creature. "Thunderer, hear me. Defender of man. Smiter of monsters. Aid me now."

The throat shifted from a tube to a sphere. A tight sphere, growing tighter all the time.

"In the beginning the monsters ran wild," Asi prayed, "and only Your divine hand preserved us. I follow in your wake."

The sphere crunched in. Cutting off Asi's air. Squeezing him until his bones began to grind. His heart pounded as though it could beat its way out through the creature. His lungs desperately seized for air that wasn't there for them.

But Asi's mind was deep in prayer. Still his lips moved as the green glow around him grew brighter. And soundlessly he said *Like You, I bind communities together. Like you, I stand against the monsters. Aid me now. Not for me, but for Thir.*

And somewhere in the skies above, the Thunderer heard him.

Within the belly of the beast, where no sound should reach, Asi heard a clap of thunder. And the moment he did, he threw every drop of power he could summon against the beast. Green fire exploding outward while the crack of thunder came down from above.

The sphere froze. Then cracked. Then split in half, dropping Asi on blackened, ruined ground as the two half of a gray granite egg rocked slowly to a stop.

Asi crawled forward until he could lay on good, healthy dirt, and collapsed. Panting gratefully for every lungful of air. His heart lurching, as though it couldn't quite believe it was still beating, and half-wanted to beat fast for the joy of it and half-wanted to slow to a speed that ensured it wouldn't burst.

It did slow, eventually. And his breaths came back at a more normal pace as well.

And finally, Asi was able to roll to his feet. He brushed leaves from his long blond hair, but did not concern himself with the ones stuck to his blue shirt or brown leather pants, much less sticking out of his heavy leather boots.

He forced himself to cross the blackened patch of dirt to find the broken, poisoned fang.

Asi gathered leaves and wove a quick pad he could use to pick up the fang without touching the poison. The poison would accumulate on the leaves, but that was well enough.

He would need that poison, and the fang, for the hardest part of this venture: breaking the curse.

And with that, Asi started back for Ulf, and then Thir.

***

As Asi rode back into town, shortly after dusk, he noted the territory marks around the Etu farm, and the surrounding farms. Especially which nearby farmer most recently seemed to claim land that had once belonged to the Etu family.

But he did not stop to deal with that. Not now.

The curse had to come first. If Asi could not break the curse, the rest ... would not matter.

Still carrying the poison fang in his hands, he rode for the center of town. It's heart. In some places it would be marked by a statue, or by the house of the founder, or perhaps the mayor.

Here in Thir, the center of town was a marketplace, all but abandoned right now. Dust and dry dirt, not even any stiff yellow grass grew here.

Only one stall was set up, and Asi could tell at a glance that it was the stall of a traveling merchant. None of the locals had enough food to sell. His stomach growled at the scent of roast chicken.

Asi noted to himself to make sure that merchant was charging a fair price. Yet one more thing to deal with, once the curse was dealt with.

Townsfolk gathered around the edges of the marketplace, but came no closer. Either fearful or respectful. The merchant began closing up shop immediately.

"You," called Asi to the merchant. "If you have been cheating these people, I will find you."

The merchant didn't answer. Only smiled and nodded as though he did not speak the local language. Asi noted the bald patch among the thatch of black hair atop his tanned scalp. Noted the wrinkles and graying whiskers. Noted the silks of his clothes, and the farmhouse drawing on his wagon.

Yes, if Asi needed to, he could find this one again.

But first, the curse.

Asi slid from his saddle in the very center of the marketplace. Ulf, having seen Asi break curses before, wisely trotted off to join the crowd at the edge of the marketplace. Although, at least, Ulf did give Asi worried glances.

At least someone would mourn him, if this did not work.

Asi lay the sopping woven pad on the ground before him, the broken fang atop it.

Asi took his two fingers of his right hand and drew a circle in the dirt around the pad. Then another, larger, around that.

Asi sat cross-legged in the outer circle.

He slammed his fist down in the dust, and a violet light flared out of him to burn like fire along the edges of both circles.

And then Asi's body slumped in place as his spirit reached past his physical confines for the spirit of the fang. While Asi's spirit looked much as his body did, down to the color of his shirt, the spirit of the fang was the whole of the granite serpent done in miniature, hissing at Asi as though laughing.

Asi grabbed the serpent in both hands.

"Fell creature," he said. "You are spent. Deceased. Nothing."

"But I *am*," it interrupted.

Asi continued the formal words of challenge to a curse spirit. "But connected to you is the curse on this land. I claim this curse is broken. I claim this curse is done. I claim this curse is over. Deny my words if you dare."

The miniature version of that great serpent – no larger now than a modest-sized garter snake – opened its mouth wide. Out poured a stream of sickly green smoke. Washing over Asi. Eating slowly away at his spirit. Burning pain spread throughout him, everywhere the smoke touched. So terrific was the pain that he could feel it reach through to his body, making it twitch and foam purple at the mouth. He could feel it trying to dry him out and force him to decay, as it had the lands and the animals of the people of Thir.

Asi reached into his core to the fire that burned at the heart of the nine parts of his spirit. One part for each of the nine worlds. One part for each of the nine tasks set before each human being, before the gates of the afterworld would swing wide to admit him after death.

And Asi met that poisonous cloud of curse with the fire of his essence.

Most curses did not require such measures. Many were little more than spells that could be unwoven or countered, with a little time and study. But this was a greater curse than any Asi had faced before. And he knew his only chance was to match power against power.

The poisonous cloud burned at him, even as the fire of his essence burned at it.

Asi held nothing back. He let his mind go blank. Forsook thoughts of home, of comfort, of the archipelago he hoped to see – everything that was for himself, Asi set aside.

He focused only on the need. On the good people of Thir. People who dug more wells than they needed, so none would have to carry water farther than they had to. Who helped each other build, and reap, and shared in such prosperity as they managed.

These people mattered. Not Asi. Not now.

And so, with all thoughts of self out of the way, the fire within Asi's soul burned hotter still. Burned away the smoke that scalded him. Burned away the sliver of serpent spirit that clung to the curse on this town.

Burned the curse itself down to ash, and that ash to nothing at all.

But such power is not tapped without price. And the moment the last of the curse burned away, Asi fell back into his body. Or rather, less of Asi fell back into his body than left it.

A ninth part of Asi's soul hovered on the brink of death. A cold pain, and a darkness that sucked Asi down.

<hr>

ASI WOKE, WHICH WAS MORE THAN HE EXPECTED. HE ACHED everywhere, even in places he hadn't known he could ache. Each beat of his heart, each slow, shallow breath, each blink of his eyes – it seemed that even things his body did without his intention carried aches.

At least he was laying on something soft. Had to be a mattress. Felt like a featherbed. Was he back in that room in the tavern, where he had lain with Kyo what seemed like a lifetime ago?

His mouth was dry, but tasted vaguely of chicken broth. He expected to smell himself. Old sweat or worse. But he didn't, which meant someone had washed him. And he could smell beeswax, which was what made him realize he could see. A dim light – still too bright right now – from two candles on the table beside him. One green, one blue.

Beeswax? Green and blue?

Asi's very eye sockets complained when he narrowed his eyes and forced them to focus on those candles. They glistened, as though oiled...

Asi sniffed the air again, checking for...there it was. Pine resin and camphor.

But who would know to—

The door opened, and Asi's beleaguered mind realized three things at the same time.

First, he was in a room with a door.

Second, this was, in fact, the room he had stayed in with Kyo.

Third, Rika had just entered the room.

She looked like the great Vana-goddess herself. Tall and fire-haired, with curves even her wolf skin cloak could not hide. Asi had seen her before, yes, at the triennial gathering, but never so close. She seemed too big for the room, as though her power pressed out upon the wooden walls and even on Asi's lungs and mouth.

At least, Asi liked to think that was the reason his breath caught.

Rika smiled, warm and welcoming as a hearth fire.

"Good," she said, "you're awake. I'd hoped to speak to you before I left."

"Left?" Asi croaked, then cleared his throat until Rika poured water from a wooden pitcher into a wooden cup, and handed him the cup. Two swallows later, he could form words.

"How long have you been here?"

"Three days." She nodded. "Long enough to ensure that Thir was doing what needed to be done for you." She smiled. "They have tended you as one of their own."

"You taught them well," Asi said, automatically, while the meaning of her words crept through his head. If they cared for him with love...

"Yes," Rika said, no doubt seeing realization spread across his face. "That ninth part of your soul is healing. Another moon and you'll be yourself again."

"*Another* moon?"

"Oh yes. You've been unconscious for some time."

"But the Etu. Their neighbors."

"Witches," said Rika. "Who made a pact with something bigger than themselves. I know. They fled the moment they were free to. The moment you broke the curse." Her expression darkened like an ice storm at sea. "I'm setting out for them now."

Asi tried to sit up, but though his neck made the effort, his torso refused to assist. He fell back into bed.

"No," said Rika. "Let me do this. Thir has been my home longer than it has been yours. Besides," – she smiled – "you've already done the hard part."

She left then, and Asi sank back into bed while he considered what Rika just said. *His home.* Thir, who had known the work of only Rika before him, now welcomed Asi as one of them. This was his home now. The first home he had made for himself outside his icy homeland.

More than he had ever dreamed of accomplishing on this trip.

The door opened again. Kyo, in her undyed cotton dress, with a smile and a bowl of soup.

"Ready to eat?" she said, and the fondness in her eye was something Asi had only ever seen back in the cold east. At the towns he had visited, Seen for, aided regularly.

To see that look here, in a place he had only been stopping on his way west, warmed him to the very core.

"Yes," he said. "Yes I am. And thank you."

SIGN UP FOR STEFON'S NEWSLETTER

Stefon loves to keep in touch with his readers, and loves to keep you reading. The best way for him to do both is for you to sign up for his newsletter.

Sign up at http://www.stefonmears.com/join

If you sign up for Stefon's newsletter, you get...

- Monthly updates about his publishing and travel schedules
- His latest news, in brief, and answers to reader questions
- A free short story for signing up
- List-only offers and occasional specials
- Plus a free short story every month!

ABOUT THE AUTHOR

Stefon Mears loves reading and writing about wizards. Stefon has more than thirty books to his credit, and he never stops writing. He earned his M.F.A. in Creative Writing from N.I.L.A., and his B.A. in Religious Studies (double emphasis in Ritual and Mythology) from U.C. Berkeley. He's a lifelong gamer and fantasy fan. Stefon lives in Portland, Oregon, with his wife and three cats.

Look for Stefon online:
www.stefonmears.com
himself@stefonmears.com